Y0-EHA-316

CE B

885 4338

SUMMER RAIN

SUMMER RAIN

•

Frances Engle Wilson

Bladen County Public Library
Elizabethtown, N. C. 28337

AVALON BOOKS

THOMAS BOUREGY AND COMPANY, INC.
401 LAFAYETTE STREET
NEW YORK, NEW YORK 10003

© Copyright 1999 by Frances Engle Wilson
Library of Congress Catalog Card Number: 98-96848
ISBN 0-8034-9337-1
All rights reserved.
All the characters in this book are fictitious,
and any resemblance to actual persons,
living or dead, is purely coincidental.

PRINTED IN THE UNITED STATES OF AMERICA
ON ACID-FREE PAPER
BY HADDON CRAFTSMEN, BLOOMSBURG, PENNSYLVANIA

To Helen, Pat, Lois, and Pam,
dedicated writers and wonderful friends.

And to Alex, the new addition to our home,
and the model for Alexander the Small.

The rain fell soft and warm the day he came,
Like tears upon his face the drops remain.
And never again will it be the same,
For three whose lives were touched by summer rain.

Chapter One

Ferns rustled gently in the languid breeze of the June afternoon, and the shady grounds surrounding the charming stone house looked lush and green. A light rain earlier in the day made the air smell fresh-washed, and there was even a clean taste to it. As Kristi approached the front porch, she saw that what had appeared from the street to be a wide, impressive front door, turned out to be two separate and quite distinctive stained wood doors with handsome decorative brass doorknobs and shield-shaped brass knocker plates. Not that double entrances were surprising, after all it was a duplex. Irene Wallace, the enthusiastic young woman at the apartment finders office, had explained this to Kristi in some detail.

1

"It's located in Marlborough, a delightful sub-urban village just twenty minutes from Philadel-phia," Irene told her. "It's a spacious, older home that the owner has renovated and remodeled into an exceptional and utterly charming two-family dwelling. The owner lives in one side and therefore he's being quite selective as to choosing a tenant for the other half. In fact, he's made so many stipulations that you're only the third person I've even considered asking him to show it to." She smiled. "Truly, it's just exceptional, and I think you'll find it's exactly what you're looking for."

"It well may be, but it sounds like the owner is either impossible to please or he's not really anx-ious to rent it to anyone," Kristi said with a dis-appointed sigh.

"Oh no. He wants it occupied all right," Irene hastened to assure her. "I believe it's that he worked so long and hard to make it into exactly the kind of lovely place it is, that now he wants to make absolutely sure he finds a responsible tenant who will appreciate and enjoy what it offers."

"Well, I can't say I blame him for that." Kristi gave Irene an agreeable nod. "At least this choosy landlord is going to let me look at his duplex. And if it's all you say it is, I'll put my best foot forward and charm the crusty ol' codger into giving me a lease." She had laughed as she'd said this, and then she'd marched out of Irene Wallace's office with a jaunty swing in her step.

Now, however, as she faced the front door that had the brass knocker with the name of COLEMAN engraved on the center, her earlier self-confident air deserted her. She hesitated for a brief moment before lifting her hand up to knock. At that same second, she heard three rapid honks of an automobile horn. She spun around to observe a shiny black car in the driveway now parking alongside her smaller white Ford Taurus. A car door flew open and a tall man jumped out.

"Hey there," he called out as he sprinted down the walk toward Kristi. "Sorry I didn't get here before you did. Got delayed at the plant, then ran into Friday afternoon traffic. I think a goodly number of Philadelphia's workforce decided to take off early so as to get a head start on the weekend." He followed his lengthy explanation with a quick laugh as he joined her on the front porch. Smiling warmly, he extended his hand. "I'm Chad Coleman, and I expect you're the person Irene Wallace sent to look at my duplex." His smiling blue eyes studied her with obvious interest, as if he found the sight of her altogether pleasing.

"That's right," she said, giving him her hand, which he immediately enclosed in a warm grasp. "I'm Kristi Saunders," she added, giving the sandy-haired young man the same interested appraisal that he'd given her. He certainly was a far cry from what she'd expected. Chad Coleman was no crusty old codger. She'd put him in the thirty-something range. He was tall with a broad chest and shoulders, strong jaw and chin, and a well-shaped mouth. At first glance she wouldn't have called him exactly handsome, though his rather rugged features were arresting, and added to that he had the most remarkable blue eyes she'd ever seen.

Kristi gave his hand a brief shake, and smiled up at him as she explained further. "The company I've been doing freelance work for has offered me a position here in Philadelphia. So I'm moving from Maryland just as soon as I find a suitable place to live."

"Well then, come take a look and see what you think of this one," Chad said, pulling a key from his pocket and unlocking the door to the left of the one that had his name on the knocker.

As the two of them stepped inside the small entry hall, Chad flipped the light switch, illuminating the decorative brass lantern-shaped light fixture that hung by a brass chain from the slightly vaulted ceiling.

"What an attractive entry," Kristi commented, taking in the creamy marble tile flooring and ivory-colored walls. "Oh, and a nice coat closet." She parted the sliding doors to discover that the inside of the closet was painted the same color as the foyer walls with a Greek key wallpaper border trim that was in black and gold. "Fancy detail—very nice."

Obviously her words pleased Chad, for he gave her an agreeing smile. "I wish I could take credit for the closet decorations, but that was the decorator's idea. I did select the floor and the wall color, however. Incidentally it's the same throughout the house, both this side and mine too. The decorator chose a color she called celery for both walls and carpet, but I stuck to my guns," he declared with a show of male pride with a bit of stubbornness added. "I liked this color," he said, pointing to the walls surrounding them. "It's called Manor White. It not only looked like the right color for my house; it sounded right as well." He made a wry face. "Who wants to see celery everywhere they look anyway?"

"A rabbit maybe," Kristi said, glancing up at him and laughing.

Now that a light, easy rapport seemed to be established between them, Chad and Kristi walked slowly through the duplex. Kristi liked the floor plan and was impressed with the size of the rooms and especially the size of the closets and the amount of shelves and cupboards both in the kitchen and in the small but adequate utility room. "I've got to tell you that whoever drew the plans

for remodeling this marvelous old house into a duplex really knew what a woman looks for in a
house.''

"Those are some of the exact words she used
to convince me to hire her.'' Chad said. "Smart
move on my part choosing a female architect,
right?'' he added with an amused smile.

"Right,'' Kristi agreed. "She did a great job for
you.''

"On the remodeling plans she was superb, I
agree a hundred percent. But she fancies herself as
something of a decorator too. On a scale of one to
ten, I only give her a five on her decorating
advice.''

Kristi narrowed her eyes at him quizzically.
"She's the one who liked celery green, I take it.''

Chad nodded. "One and the same.'' He
laughed, and Kristi enjoyed watching his face. He
had a nice mouth, firm but kind.

At this time they were just walking into the last
room, which was a small, corner room at the back
that could serve as a second bedroom or a study.
Seeing it, Kristi could hardly contain her delight.
Being a corner room, there were windows on two
sides letting in lots of light. It would make an absolutely perfect place for her to work in. Though
it was of modest size, still there was ample room
to set up her drawing board and her big flat-top
desk and the cupboard with her sketch pads, paints,

and all her drawing equipment. "I could sure put a light, bright room like this to good use. I come up with my best drawings and ideas when I work alone at home. I could really be creative here." Kristi voiced her thoughts with enthusiasm.

Chad gave her a speculative look. "Sounds like you're an artist of some kind."

"Artist is a grand-scale title. I simply design greeting cards and draw a cartoon now and then."

"Hey, you mean you make those cards that the people flip over to see the crown on the back?" An arched eyebrow indicated his humorous surprise.

She smiled. "Actually, I have sold some designs to Hallmark while I was freelancing. However, the company that's bringing me to Philadelphia is Word Wise Card Company."

"That sounds like a neat job. I bet you're plenty good at it too."

"I'm not too shabby," she quipped. Then, before he could question her further about her work, she started walking out of the room. "Let's go outside now. I'm eager to see what your yard is like," she said, as she walked with purposeful steps into the kitchen and through the sliding glass doors that opened onto a long porch. The design of the eight-foot-deep porch was simple and classic, with white columns supporting the roof. The porch stretched across the entire back of the house, providing ample room for an array of patio furniture for seating and dining. At Chad's end of the porch was a charcoal broiler and other outdoor cooking equipment.

"I see that you're something of an outside chef, and you certainly have created the perfect yard for outdoor entertaining." Kristi's voice mirrored her enthusiastic approval as she looked out over the backyard, taking in the appealing assortment of shrubbery and perennials that thrived beneath the shade of several large trees.

"I hardly rate the title of chef," Chad said with a diffident shrug. "I'm just your ordinary backyard barbecuer. I do grill a pretty fair hamburger, though." A slow grin spread across his face. "I think what really sold me on this house in the first place was the yard and these beautiful old trees. Then when we started planning the renovations, I knew that to fully enjoy the trees and yard I needed the addition of the ideal type of porch. Voilà! There it is!" He waved his arm in a sweeping gesture. "I'm no architect, but I'd say I designed a first-rate addition to this place of mine."

"You sure did," Kristi agreed heartily.

"Not too shabby for a chemical engineer—right?" he quipped, giving her a broad wink.

Kristi laughed. "Right," she said, studying him with a quizzical look, narrrowing her eyes. *So he's a chemical engineer.* Discovering this about Chad

Coleman both surprised and interested her. She'd figured that he was a building contractor, or had a construction company of some kind. It seemed logical to her that he worked in some area that went along with this desire of his to tackle the remodeling of an old house. Obviously he was a man of multiple interests and abilities. This impressed her. To Kristi, anyone who could master chemistry had to be as intelligent as a Rhodes scholar. Even with the aid of a tutor, she'd barely managed to pass the simplest basic chemistry course required in order to graduate from her high school. Recalling that now, she grimaced inwardly.

"In fact, I'd say what you've accomplished with all of it, both inside and out, is terrific. It's exactly right for me, and as for Alex, though he's tolerated apartment living, he's never liked it. This yard of yours would be heaven to him." She hastened to add this with a show of enthusiasm.

Frowning, Chad studied her with a speculative look. "You know, when Irene Wallace called me about showing the duplex, she just gave me your name, Kristi Saunders. She didn't mention that you were married and that it was a couple who was interested in my place."

She gaped at him, flabbergasted by his words. "I'm not married. Why would you think that?" she cried, her voice echoing incredulity.

"But then you're planning on having someone

share the duplex with you—isn't that right?'' He was studying her now with a curious intensity.

''No, of course it isn't.'' Kristi shook her head at him. ''Absolutely not!'' she declared emphatically. ''If you'll allow me to rent it, I can assure you that I'll be living here solo. I can't imagine where you got the idea I'd have someone living here with me.'' She squared her shoulders and put her hands on her hips. ''I'm independent. I can live very well by myself,'' she added with a slight smile of defiance.

''But you did mention this Alex and how he would enjoy the yard—''

''Yes, I know I did,'' she said, interrupting him. ''Of course Alex will be here with me. That goes without saying. He's a major part of my life. He's my good-luck charm. Why Alexander gave me my career.'' Suddenly in her outpouring of words, a dreadful thought occurred to Kristi. She stopped short, gazing at Chad, a look of anguish in her eyes. ''Oh golly, please don't tell me you won't allow a dog.'' Kristi didn't pause to let him answer. ''Now truly, Alexander is so well-behaved, and he's quiet. Why, you'll scarcely know he's around, and he won't cause anybody any trouble. I promise you that. Besides, he's not a large dog, he only weighs about twenty pounds. That's the reason for his name. He couldn't be Alexander the Great, so of course everybody knows him as

Alexander the Small.'' She rattled off all this as if her words were completely logical and coherent.

Chad looked at her with amused wonder. ''I don't know how it could be possible, but I think all you've been saying is starting to make sense to me.'' He chuckled, folding his arms across his chest. ''Why didn't you tell me that your career includes more than just greeting cards?''

''I think I mentioned drawing a cartoon now and then.''

''Look, I get the daily newspaper, and *Alexander the Small* is no now and then cartoon.'' He took a step closer, inclining his head and smiling. ''Now in answer to your question as to if I allow dogs or not, I most certainly would welcome Alex. He's a celebrity and so is his creator, and who could ask for any more interesting tenants than that? I'd say you and I have a deal,'' Chad said, smiling with satisfaction.

''We have indeed,'' Kristi responded, exhaling a sigh of contentment. If she'd been alone, she would have jumped up and down and shouted because of this stroke of good luck. She gloried over the fact of gaining this ideal duplex for herself and a fenced-in and tree-filled yard for Alex. In the bargain, she'd gotten a new landlord who was full of surprises to say the very least. For Chad Coleman was turning out to have as many facets to him as a well-cut jewel. He was a chemical engineer, a sometimes architect, a master of the outdoor charcoal broiler, a discerning cartoon reader, and a dog lover. Now even if he should turn out to be a so-so sort of landlord, he'd still get an A-1 rating from her.

Chapter Two

Kristi didn't waste a minute before setting the wheels in motion in order to move from Maryland to Pennsylvania within the following week. The distance between Baltimore and Philadelphia was only about a hundred miles, so that facilitated things to a degree.

The morning after Chad had rented her the duplex, she was driving the interstate before nine o'clock. She made a brief stop at the kennels where she'd boarded Alex, and the two of them walked into her apartment building in Baltimore at ten minutes after eleven. By midafternoon Kristi had the place strewn with cardboard boxes, each one of which Alex had to fully investigate, first by sniffing around the outside and then by trying to knock each one over so he could nose around the contents and find some article he could drag out.

It took several firm reprimands from her, as well as the substitution of a beef jerky dog treat for Kristi to retrieve her sheepskin, and finally convince Alex that all articles placed in a packing box were to remain *in the box*.

On the following Tuesday morning, the movers arrived at precisely seven forty-five, as promised. The two tall, sturdy men made an efficient working team. They had her apartment emptied and the moving van loaded before noon. Since they informed Kristi that they would stop for lunch before setting out for Marlborough, she and Alex left immediately in order to get to the duplex well ahead of them.

Kristi's spirits were high as she drove away from Baltimore. And even Alex seemed to sense that he was setting off on a new adventure. It was a perfect, warm day. A gentle wind was stirring the June green foliage which had begun to thicken on the trees, and the japonica and laurel bushes were in blossom. All of a sudden she was recalling something she'd read somewhere about this first month of summer. It was that June was like a girl on the brink of new adventure, with a short past behind her and her future ahead. And June may open many doors to one who walks through her shining days with her hopes high, and with her heart on tiptoe. She smiled to herself, for it was such a lovely thought.

The remainder of the day went well. Due to the good-natured attitude of the two moving men and their seemingly tireless energy, they had her moved in with her furniture in place and most everything in good order by late that afternoon. Outside, the summer sun had begun its downward slide. The oak trees in the backyard cast long shadows across the grass. Kristi paused in the shade of the wide porch and turned her face toward the cool breeze that came whispering through the trees, letting its freshness soothe and refresh her. Alex, who had been scouting the perimeters of the yard, was now beginning to investigate each flower, shrub, and tree. Kristi leaned her back against one of the white wooden columns to rest and enjoy the sunset. The sun at that moment was poised on the edge of the horizon, a fat red ball that cast a ruddy shimmer for a few minutes before it rolled over the edge of the world and was gone. But the whole of the west was drenched with the scarlet splash of that plunge, and there were streaks of bloody gold along the horizon to north and south.

''Oh, there you are.'' Chad strode out of his back door onto the porch. ''I knocked on your front door, but when you didn't answer I figured you might be out here. I noticed Alexander earlier before the van left.''

"Yeah, he's been going in and out all afternoon. He's completely enchanted by his new domain. Aren't you, Alex?" At the sound of his name, Alex bounded up the steps, wagging his tail and eyeing Chad in friendly speculation. He didn't approach Chad however, but sat down next to the column where Kristi stood.

"You're a winning little fellow," Chad said warmly, leaning over and cocking his head at Alex. "I've seen a lot of you in the newspaper and I'm happy now to get to know you in the flesh."

Alex didn't understand Chad's words of course, but he reacted to the friendly tone of Chad's voice and his manner with more vigorous tail-wagging.

Chad patted the little dog's head, then straightened up and turned his attention again to Kristi. "I saw the moving van pulling off and I thought maybe I could help you hook up some of your appliances. I'm a do-it-yourself handyman, not terribly skilled, but I work for free," he said, giving her a sudden crinkly grin that was compelling and boyish.

A faint smile curved the line of her lips with softness. "I sure appreciate the offer, and the price is certainly right. But the moving guys took care of my washer and dryer. In fact, I'm in good shape, and everything is operable except for my telephone, and they're supposed to come out first thing tomorrow to install that."

"Well, feel free to use my phone tonight if you need to."

"Thanks, but all I want to do is unpack boxes of dishes and the stuff to put my kitchen in order. After that I'm just going to call it a day and fall in bed." She followed this statement with a weary sigh, and at the same time brushed back soft curling wisps of cinnamon-brown hair from her forehead.

"Look, there's got to be some little thing I can do to help you." Chad narrowed his eyes thoughtfully. "I'll tell you what. You get started on your kitchen and I'll fire up the grill and cook you some dinner."

"You don't need to bother with me," she protested.

"Hey, it's no bother. I'm going to be cooking for myself anyway. I'll just stick on a couple of extra pieces of chicken, another ear of corn, and slice up some tomatoes and green stuff. How does that sound to you?"

"Absolutely super!" A swift smile parted her lips and made her green eyes sparkle with pleasure. Kristi had beautiful eyes that often held a glint of humor and a hint of fire. They were shot with intelligence and their verdant color was splashed with bronze, like the trefoil of the real Irish shamrock. "And, I might add, a real lifesaver. I was going to have to settle for a dinner of canned soup and a few graham crackers. Because after the long day I've had, I'm too tired to go hunt up a grocery store, and what food I moved from my apartment in Baltimore consists of two cans of soup, one of sliced peaches, and a case of Alpo dog food.'' She related these sad details to Chad in a woe-is-me tone of voice, but that glint of humor remained in her eyes.

"Well, I'm glad I could rescue you from your grim plight,'' he said, laughing in a jovial way.

"Me too,'' she quipped, turning and taking a step toward her open sliding glass door. "I'll be right inside here in my kitchen. You just give me a holler when you want me.''

"Okay, I'd guess that would be about an hour and a quarter from now, if that's agreeable.''

She bobbed her head. "You bet. That's great.'' She waved him off and went inside.

With a burst of renewed energy, Kristi ripped the sealing tape off of the cartons that held her china and glassware and began to arrange her kitchen cabinets. As she worked, she was thinking what a pleasant sort of guy Chad Coleman seemed to be. It was a nice gesture on his part to offer her a helping hand. She appreciated it.

When she started to tackle the two cartons that held pots and pans and kitchen utensils, her interest in this job definitely started to wane. Maybe it was the silence around her that made it so dreary.

A little upbeat music would prove welcome about now to spur her on. She frowned, remembering that her tapes, compact discs, as well as her transistor radio were all still locked up in the trunk of her car. "Wouldn't you know it," she muttered with a disgusted shrug. Well, she sure couldn't take time to go get them out now. If she had any time to spare at all before Chad called her to dinner, she needed to use it to wash up a little and at least put on lipstick and comb her hair. This thought caused her to look down at the somewhat grungy Reeboks, faded jeans, and less than pristine yellow polo shirt she was wearing. The wear and tear of this long day didn't add favorably to her appearance either. No wonder her new neighbor and landlord had taken pity on her. No one looked more like they needed a care package than she did.

By this time, Kristi was down to unpacking the final box, which held small electrical appliances like her toaster, steam iron, electric mixer, and can opener. Seeing the can opener reminded her that she needed to open a can of dog food and feed Alex. Poor little guy, it was already more than an hour later than the time she normally fed him. It surprised her that he hadn't come begging by this time, because she had left the sliding glass door open so he could come in and out while all the moving was going on. As Kristi approached the open door to call Alex, she heard a woman's agitated voice.

"Honestly, Chad, I simply can't believe that you've been foolish enough to lease the duplex to people with a scruffy nuisance of a dog. I suppose they also have a noisy child to bother us as well."

Kristi didn't wait to hear Chad's reply. She gave a quick whistle. "Come Alex," she called out sharply. "Chow time."

Alex bounded across the porch, and the instant he was inside, Kristi slid the door shut, immediately flipping the lock with trembling fingers. There was a tightening of the lines that ran from her nostrils to the corners of her mouth that betrayed her inner tensions. She was more than a little upset about what she'd just overheard. Who was this woman who objected to both dogs and children? Was she Chad's business associate? Some fellow chemist?, Or possibly his girlfriend? This thought caused feelings of uneasiness to tug at the corners of her mind. If she were someone important to him, her attitude could make Chad Coleman regret accepting Kristi as a tenant. On this sour note, Kristi heaved a ragged sigh. Hopefully Chad's complaining friend would prove to be an infrequent visitor. But Kristi had a strong suspicion that the opposite was more likely to be the case.

It was fifteen minutes later when Chad rapped

on Kristi's door. "Come on, neighbor, dinner's ready and waiting," he yelled, continuing to tap away on the glass until she got there to undo the lock.

Although Kristi felt like it wasn't much of an improvement, she had combed her hair and changed into a fresh, light blue shirt. She was glad she'd done this when Chad gave her an approving glance.

"You've got that satisfied, mission-accomplished look in your eyes," he said as they walked across to his side of the porch. "I take it that you got your kitchen all put in order."

Kristi nodded. "Yeah, I did. Actually, except for getting rid of all the empty cartons, I have everything in pretty good shape now."

"Say, that's plenty good. And as to the boxes, if you'll stash them out by the garage, I'll arrange with Eric to haul them off. He'll do it on Thursday when he picks up Greta." As Chad told her this, he seated her in one of the cushioned metal chairs pulled up to the round patio table. Two places were set at the table, with wooden bowls of green salad and tall glasses of iced tea.

"Eric? Greta?" There were question marks in Kristi's voice. "Clue me in on them, won't you?"

Chad was busy lifting chicken off the grill with a pair of tongs. He cast a quick look over his shoulder at Kristi. "I'll tell you all about them in a minute.'' He turned back and added an ear of corn and a thick slice of garlic bread to each of their plates and carried them to the table.

''Umm—this looks and smells wonderful. And I've never been hungrier,'' she stated emphatically. ''Actually, this will be my first sit-down meal today. I've been too busy to take time out to eat.''

''Well you can now, so chow down and enjoy.''

She gave a quick laugh. ''I've already started,'' she quipped, gaily, as she began sprinkling salt and pepper on her ear of corn and gnawing off a mouthful.

Chad was obviously pleased that she relished every bite she put in her mouth. ''I like a girl who eats with gusto,'' he said.

''Then you're really going to like me,'' she mocked playfully.

''I have no doubt of that,'' he countered, looking across the table at her in his direct, serious way. ''None at all.'' His gaze was contemplative.

Kristi took a quiet moment to look back at him. He smiled then, and the allure in his eyes took her breath away. She quickly shifted her attention again to her food. ''Tell me about this Eric and Greta now,'' she said, picking up her knife and fork to start eating her chicken.

''They're a Pennsylvania Dutch couple who live over in Chester County. Greta comes on Thursday to clean my place, and while she's here she fixes me some great food. You've heard what good cooks the Pennsylvania Dutch women are, I'm sure. Well Greta is a prime example. Her sausages and dumplings are sensational, and her shoofly pie you'll have to sample for yourself. It's tasty." He smacked his lips.

"You make her sound almost too good to be true."

"She is special all right. She's neat as a pin, pleasant as pie, and has a face as round as a plate, and a heart as full of sunshine as a hayfield."

Kristi smiled. "You paint a nice picture of her. Now tell me all about Eric."

"He's something of a character, tough as a hickory rail, and looks somewhat like Abraham Lincoln. And he never met a stranger. He's friendly as a warm handshake."

"You certainly describe them in colorful terms. I think I may want to use them on a greeting card sometime." She reached for her iced tea and asked, "What does Eric do?"

"He runs a mushroom farm in Kennett Square."

She cocked her head at him, frowning. "You're kidding me, aren't you?"

Chad shook his head. "Growing mushrooms is big business here. Don't you know that Pennsylvania is the leading producer of mushrooms in the nation?"

"Being from as near by as Maryland, I suppose I should have known that, but I didn't." She pretended to be shamefaced by her lack of knowledge.

"I'll tell you what. Next Sunday, if you're free, we could take a drive through the area surrounding the town of Kennett Square and you'll not only see the mushroom farms, you'll smell the fusty scent they lend to the countryside."

"Sounds sort of interesting, but I don't know about that fusty odor bit. Isn't that like a moldy mildew smell?"

Chad shrugged. "I guess that's one way to describe it. To me it's like the stale odor of an old wooden barrel."

She wrinkled her nose in distaste. "Somehow that doesn't sound one bit appetizing to me."

"It's rather intriguing once you get used to it. Besides, the mushrooms are fantastic. They're a tan color that's almost white, and they grow very big. When you get them freshly picked, they're incredibly good, and they can range in size from about the size of a silver dollar to that of one of my mother's best china saucers." He leaned forward inclining his head closer to hers. "I just thought of something. I bet if you'd let me show you this area, you could use it in one of your Alexander the Small cartoons. Think about Alexander sniffing the musty smells and peeking under

Bladen County Public Library
Elizabethtown, N. C. 28337

a big mushroom to discover what was hiding under such a strange sort of umbrella.''

Intrigued and a bit amazed that Chad would relate to her career like this, she eyed him thoughtfully. ''You know, you've given me an idea that has great possibilities. I like it,'' she declared with an emphatic bob of her head. Kristi hesitated, scrutinizing Chad intently. ''Tell me honestly, would you mind if we took Alex along with us Sunday?''

''Of course not,'' he answered without a second of hesitation.

She didn't hide her pleasure. ''Thanks,'' she said, smiling across the table at him. ''You're a nice, clever guy, and you've started me thinking about several cartoons that could develop from Alexander's adventures in *The mushroom capital of the world.* If that happens, then I'll owe you for giving me the idea. What kind of commission do you ask?''

''I'm very negotiable,'' he said, a mischievous gleam of interest in his blue eyes. He didn't elaborate on this, he simply looked at her and smiled. It was not a wide smile, but there was something about it that was oddly appealing, and it did unruly things to her heart.

This man was a charmer all right, and as enticing as a riddle, she thought, reaching for her glass and drinking some of her iced tea. She cautioned herself to remember that he was also her landlord. He simply was trying to establish a pleasant, friendly rapport with his tenant, nothing more.

Chapter Three

The rest of the week sped by as Kristi settled into her work routine at Word Wise. She had been doing fairly well freelancing and hadn't sought out this job. It was Word Wise that had come seeking her. They made a highly attractive offer to get her to join their company, and to cinch the deal they told her they wanted her to design a line of greeting cards with Alexander the Small. Word Wise executives were convinced that Alexander the Small greeting cards had great potential. "Another company may have Garfield, but we here at Word Wise will have Alexander." These were the company president's impassioned words.

On Friday morning, Kristi was at the drawing board sketching the designs for the first two

Alexander cards. Rain was pattering against the office windows in the room where she was working. It was a pleasant sound. She looked up from her work to watch as fat, clumsy drops ran down the glass, and through streaks of falling drops a tiny rainbow webbed its way onto the plate glass and formed a delicate prism in the corner of the pane.

The rain had picked up by lunchtime. Kristi ordered in a sandwich and a milk shake, ate quickly, then returned to her drawing board.

Throughout the entire day the rain continued— like a child that goes on crying, too tired and inert to stop. The sky was a pale washed-out blue when she left at five o'clock, and everything looked wet and shining, translucent in the summer light.

As she started the drive from Philadelphia to Marlborough, the summer rain was falling through the trees with a gentle whispering sound. The rumble of the city continued to come faintly on the wind, blown like a mist from the drenched streets. However, by the time she reached the outlying suburban villages, the rain had almost stopped. But drops of water continued to play down from the wet leaves of the tall trees.

When she arrived at the duplex, she ran her car into her side of the garage. Chad's side was empty. His car had not been there for the past three days. In fact, Kristi hadn't seen him since the night she'd moved in, when he'd cooked dinner for her. She supposed he'd gone out of town. She guessed that Greta and Eric had been there, because the packing boxes she'd stashed at the side of the garage were gone when she got home from work on Thursday. All she really knew was that she'd not seen or heard anything from Chad's side during the past three days. She looked at his empty side of the garage, ending her conjecturing with a shrug of her shoulders. What Chad did with his days and nights was of no concern to her. They shared a duplex. This made them neighbors—and neighbors should respect each other's privacy. With this in mind, Kristi closed the garage door and strode purposefully to her front door.

Once inside, she went directly to the sliding glass doors to let Alex in. Usually, the minute he heard her car go in the garage he came to the back door and started barking and pawing the glass, so it surprised her that today he wasn't there waiting to come in.

Kristi stepped outside. "Here Alex, come here boy," she called, clapping her hands to get his attention.

Alex came bounding across from Chad's side of the porch. It was then that Kristi saw that there was a little boy huddled up on the long lounge chair. He wore faded jeans and a blue denim jacket, equally faded. He had his knees pulled up to his chin, hugging them as though he were trying to hold himself together, to keep from falling apart.

"Hi there," Kristi greeted him, walking over to him. "You look like you got caught out in the rain. You're wet as a fish." She gave him a caring smile. "What can I do to help you?"

"Nothin'," he said, his peacock-blue eyes squinting from tears. "I gotta wait here for somebody."

Kristi felt a soft rush of pity for the sad little guy. She scrutinized his face, trying to determine how old he might be. She'd guess seven, maybe eight. He had a grave, heart-shaped face wide across his cheekbones, and his appealing big eyes were intriguingly outlined as if by a crayon, with short black eyelashes. His hair was pale brown, the way sand looks on a beach after the water has poured over it, and it stood up on end like the soft thick hair on the face of a terrier—much like Alex's for that matter. She smiled at the thought.

"How long have you been waiting now?" she asked, thinking if she could get some information out of him maybe she could be of some help.

"I don't know. Pretty long time, I guess. The truck driver let me out this morning up that way, by the mall. I walked the rest of the way here. It was raining kinda hard. That's how I got wet," he explained, his hands moving in helpless, childish gestures as he talked.

"That's quite a ways to walk—especially in the rain. How come the truck didn't bring you down here?"

"He was in a big hurry, I guess. He said he didn't have time to bother with me anymore, and since I'd been here before and knew the way, I could just go along by myself."

A shadow of surprise crossed Kristi's face. "You've been here to this house before?"

"Sure have." He bobbed his head affirmatively. "I always visit in the summer, and I'm going to stay a long while with him this time. There was a quick spark of eagerness in his eyes as he declared this fact.

Completely nonplussed to hear the boy say this, Kristi scrutinized his intent little face, with a questioning look. She took note of the vivid color of his eyes, the sandy shade of his hair, and his small straight nose with the suggestion of an upward tilt at the tip. Certainly there were some similarities in his features to those of Chad. His heart-shaped face, however, he must have taken from his mother. His sudden presence on Chad's back porch began to make sense now. Apparently he was Chad's son, and he spent time in the summer, when there was no school, with his father, and the rest of the time lived some other place with his mother. But if this were true, why on earth wasn't Chad here to meet his son when he arrived? And why was this boy brought to Marlborough and dropped off like a piece of freight at a shopping mall? What sort of parent could be that irresponsible and uncaring about his own child as to permit this to happen? Kristi's expressive face tightened in anger as she thought of all the trouble and disappointment this young boy had endured throughout this day.

"Hey, I've just thought of what you and I can do while we wait for Chad to get home." She held out her hand to him. "I'm Kristi. What's your name?"

"Mickey." He tugged at his lip with his teeth, then added. "It's really Michael, but I like Mickey best."

"That's like me," she told him. "Mine is really Kristen, but I like Kristi best." They exchanged a brief smile. "So Mickey, while we wait, why don't you come into my house and let me fix us some supper. After a day in the rain I bet you're hungry, aren't you?"

He bobbed his head. "Yeah, I am."

"And I also bet you've got a dry pair of jeans and a shirt in that bag over there." She pointed to a canvas backpack deposited outside Chad's back door.

He bobbed his head affirmatively again. Then he got up out of the chair and smiled for the first time, a sort of crooked little smile that was funny and young and appealing. As he walked over to collect his gear, he said, ''Could we leave a note for him, so he'll know where to find me?''

''Sure, that's a good idea. You can put notes on both his front and back doors with some Scotch tape just as soon as you've changed into dry clothes. Then he'll be sure to see it first thing when he comes home.''

The rain had ended, but the cloudy gray sky gave off only a murky light, making the end of the day more than a little somber. Kristi was quick to switch on the kitchen lights as she led Mickey inside. She immediately pointed out the way to the bathroom, and after providing him with a clean towel and washcloth, she left him alone to wash up and change his clothes.

While he did this, she flipped on the table lamps in the living room and turned on the stereo. The soft amber glow of light and the pleasant sound of the theme music from *The Lion King* she hoped would make her young guest feel welcome.

She hurried into her kitchen to try to figure out what she should feed Chad's son for supper. When she was driving home from work, that afternoon, she had planned on having a curried chicken salad for her dinner. But that was hardly suitable for a young, growing boy, who more than likely had not had anything to eat since breakfast. What, she wondered, do kids his age like to eat anyway?

Probably pizzas or hamburgers with french fries. She groaned at this thought. For even though she'd shopped at two supermarkets on Wednesday to stockpile her new kitchen and her freezer, she had not purchased these items.

Opening the freezer compartment of the refrigerator, she scanned her selection of frozen dinners. The choice was limited, and her decision was quick. She pulled out spaghetti with meatballs for Mickey, lasagna for herself. Noticing that she had cartons of both chocolate and butter pecan ice cream encouraged her. That plus chocolate chip cookies without a doubt would make an acceptable dessert to finish off with.

By the time Mickey came back from sticking the notes he'd printed on Chad's doors, Kristi had their supper on the dining room table.

"Gee, that tasted good," he quickly exclaimed, after devouring his supper. He offered Kristi a small, shy smile as he added, "Thanks a lot."

"You're certainly welcome, Mickey." She smiled back at him. "Now how does ice cream and cookies sound for dessert?"

"All right!" he answered, his smile growing into a jack-o'-lantern grin.

It was sometime after eight o'clock that evening when Chad appeared at Kristi's front door. Beaming with joy, Mickey bounded across the living room and hurled himself into Chad's outstretched arms. "You're here—you got home," he squealed excitedly, as Chad lifted him off the floor in a bear hug.

"I'm here, all right. I just got off the plane from Chicago in fact. And what a surprise to find you here. I had no idea you were coming. What's up, anyway? Where's Jack?"

"He's gone somewhere. He said he'd be away a long time, too." A shadow flitted across the boy's face, obliterating his earlier smile.

Chad frowned. "Why didn't he let me know? Doesn't he realize that I always want to be right here when you come?"

"He was in a hurry. I guess he forgot." There was a tremor in his voice as if he were fighting back tears.

"Well, I got back and we're together now. That's the good part. So everything is okay now, isn't it, fella?" Chad set him down, but kept one arm around his shoulders as he looked over Mickey's head to speak to Kristi. "I'm sorry about putting you to all this trouble. It's totally reprehensible of Jack to have done this, and there's no excuse for someone letting this happen," he said fiercely. "I hate to think of Mickey waiting here alone and scared. I can't thank you enough for looking after him like you have." Chad's earnest eyes sought hers. "You're a real guardian angel," he said, as his eyes bathed her in admiration.

Chad had Mickey gather up his things then, and the two of them immediately went home to Chad's side of the duplex. Kristi wasted no time in finishing the remaining chores. She cleared the dining room table, started the dishwasher, and quickly put the kitchen in spic and span order.

She'd been going in high gear ever since she'd gotten home and found a rain-soaked boy on Chad's porch. Now that she was alone, she wanted to relax and take time to assimilate all that had occurred. Heading now into her bedroom, she undressed quickly and put on her favorite apple green, cotton-knit sleep shirt. She then returned to the living room to curl up on the sofa and watch television while Alex snoozed on the cool marble floor in the entry hall.

As she randomly punched different channel buttons on the remote, hunting for a program that would appeal to her, she recalled what Chad had said about there being no excuse for someone sending Mickey to stay with him without informing him when the boy was coming. By *someone*, Kristi presumed Chad meant Mickey's mother. But who was this Jack that Chad had angrily questioned Mickey about? Had Chad's wife remarried, and was Jack Mickey's stepfather? That was a possible explanation, and could account for Chad's animosity. Kristi couldn't help being extremely curious about all of this. Because for some reason that she couldn't quite put her finger on, she got the feeling that it might be different from the way it seemed.

She was still contemplating this thought when she heard the first rumble of thunder, arriving stealthily, gathering sonorous momentum, and finally tearing mightily through the night's silence. Silver lightning then slashed the velvet darkness, and moments later the summer rain began pouring down again.

Chapter Four

Kristi had mapped out a number of chores she wanted to accomplish on Saturday. First of all, while it was still early, she showered and then wrapped a towel, turban-style, around her just-washed hair. Next, she immediately put her week's laundry into the washing machine, including the jeans and shirt that Mickey had worn in the rain. She ate her breakfast while the clothes were washing, and once she had them in the dryer, she used her blow-dryer on her hair and then relaxed with her second cup of coffee.

It was while she was folding the laundry and putting it away that she took a closer look at Mickey's clothes. The jeans were of poor-quality denim, cheaply made, and the seat was worn thin so you could almost see light through it, and there were frazzled tears on both knees. The shirt was not any better. It was made of a flimsy polyester and cotton blend, and originally it was probably a bright red and blue plaid, but now it was dull-colored and had buttons missing. She knew the kids today were into the grunge look, with bleached streaked jeans and unironed shirts, but these clothes of Mickey's went beyond grunge. Surely his mother could afford nicer clothes than these for her son. It seemed incongruous that Mickey was sent to visit his father in clothes that made him look like some orphaned waif. And even stranger than what he was wearing was the fact that instead of being put on a plane or a bus, it would seem he was given a ride by some trucker. The whole thing was bizarre to say the least. She sighed, shrugging her shoulders as she set Mickey's things aside, ready to return to him. Then she turned her thoughts to her most important Saturday project, which was choosing the perfect wall area to hang each of her collected art treasures.

Being an artist of sorts herself, Kristi had a strong interest as well as a cultivated appreciation of good art. She made a hobby of attending art shows, visiting galleries, and occasionally taking in one of the auction sales. Four years ago, when her Alexander the Small cartoons became syndicated, she decided she could at last indulge her hobby and search in earnest for paintings that had strong appeal for her, and buy those that she could afford. To date, she had purchased two quite lovely watercolors by a well-known Japanese artist, a charming, small oil painting of two barefoot children gathering shells along a seashore by a contemporary Cape Cod painter, and her most prized acquisition, a large, Southwestern landscape by Clark Hulings.

It took her some time. When she had all four paintings placed, she stood back admiring them, experiencing a glow of satisfaction. She had put the finishing touch to her new home. Every room now bore her personal mark, reflecting her taste, her style, even her personality.

Maybe it was because she'd been working with her little art collection today, or possibly she'd had it in the back of her mind all along. At any rate, later that afternoon she decided to look into an art sale that one of the people at Word Wise had mentioned. They'd said that the old Liberty Gallery had recently been taken over by a new owner. The name had been changed to the Trevor Gallery and a big sale was in progress to reduce the old inventory. It was reported that there were some true bargains to be had. Kristi couldn't resist such a temptation. Some gallery sales are rather classy affairs, others are casual, with almost a flea market atmosphere. Not knowing what the staus would be in Philadelphia, Kristi dressed in a sporty beige summer suit, a pair of comfortable, low-heeled pumps, and slung a tan leather bag over her shoulder after she'd tucked a checkbook into one of the zipper compartments. Then, as soon as she'd turned Alex into the backyard with a bowl of fresh water and a handful of dog treats, she headed into the city.

She had a general idea of the area of Philadelphia she was looking for, and with the help of the street map, she had little trouble locating the Trevor Gallery.

As she entered the Colonial-style building, two men were leaving, both carrying paintings under their arms. This would indicate that the sale was going rather well. The fact that there was a good-sized crowd browsing around inside also confirmed this. It appeared to be a fair-sized gallery. Kristi took her time wandering slowly through the various rooms, carefully examing any painting that attracted even a casual interest. She'd learned from experience that it pays to evaluate a work of art from several angles and without haste.

She had been in the gallery a little over an hour when she glimpsed an oil painting that almost took her breath away. It was entitled *Flower Piece*, and was a painting of a bouquet of flowers in a crystal vase. The vase was set atop a hexagon-shaped mahogany table placed in front of a wide window.

Beyond the window could be seen the distant vista of a river, spanned by a high bridge shrouded in mist. The artist had painted the flowers with a delicate, ethereal grace that had an unsubstantial air of lightness, anchored to reality by the bowl-shaped glass vase. The lightness of tone combined with lightness of touch was the keynote of the picture. To Kristi it almost seemed as if a gust of wind from the river would scatter the contents of the bowl in a flurry of petals.

Being so taken up with her study of this painting, she was unaware that two people had come up to stand behind her until she felt a hand on her shoulder and heard Chad's warm baritone voice.

"Hi neighbor, this is certainly a nice surprise finding you here. Mickey and I had reservations about coming to an art sale, but running into you makes it all better. Doesn't it, Mick?" Chad glanced down at the boy standing beside him. "See, I told you something good might happen before this day was over."

"I'd say from the sharp way you're dressed, Mickey, that something good has already happened," Kristi said, giving him an admiring glance. "Aren't those brand-new jeans you're wearing?"

"Yeah, and these are new too." He pointed to his black and white athletic shoes. "Aren't these supercool?"

"Absolutely *the coolest*," she affirmed strongly.

"I've got on everything new," Mickey declared proudly. Chad said I needed everything from the skin out. Didn't you?"

Chad chuckled. "Well, I did feel that replenishing your wardrobe was the first order of the day. Don't you agree, Kristi?" He gave her an amused wink.

"Totally," she said with conviction. After her first-hand examination of the clothes he'd arrived in, Kristi couldn't agree more. He not only needed nice new clothes, he needed personal attention and the kind of fatherly concern that Chad so obviously was eager to provide. As she continued to admire the small boy's well-groomed appearance, she didn't have to guess that the first stop he and Chad had made this morning was the barber shop. For Mickey's shaggy, unruly hair had been well cut and tamed down just the right amount to give him that good, all-American boy look that is so appealing in those television ads for Miracle Whip salad dressing and Oscar Mayer weiners.

Chad must have felt that the subject of Mickey's new clothes had been adequately covered. "We mustn't keep you from your enjoyment of the gallery," he said. "And we need to find Sybil Trevors and talk with her for a few minutes anyway."

"Well, you're not interfering with me at all. In fact, I've decided to buy this flower painting," she gestured toward the one she'd chosen. "I just need to find someone who can lift it down off the wall for me, and then tell me where to go to pay for it."

"You're in luck. I see Sybil heading our way right now. She owns the gallery and she'll see to everything for you." Chad waved his hand in the direction of the woman who was coming through the arched doorway at the far end of the room.

Kristi watched as a beautiful woman with red hair cropped short and a delicate profile atop a long, lean, dancer's body walked toward the corner of the room where they were standing. She was wearing a black skirt and a white silk shirt with a string of pearls looped low over the neckline. Black high-heeled shoes added to her height and showed off her slim calves and narrow ankles.

"Here you are, Chad. I've been looking for you. One of my assistants said she noticed you come in. I was with a customer, but I came as soon as I could get away. You're here earlier than I expected. You know, of course, that I won't be leaving the gallery until after five. I trust you made our dinner reservations for seven or later." She looked straight at Chad as if he were the only one there as she said all of this.

"We'll discuss dinner later," Chad interjected. "Right now I want you to meet Kristi Saunders, who incidentally wishes to purchase a painting from you. Kristi this is Sybil, she owns Trevor Gallery.''

Sybil acknowledged the introduction, eyeing Kristi with interest and offering a courteous smile. ''That's nice to hear, of course. So tell me, which painting is it that you've selected?''

''This one hanging on the wall behind me,'' Kristi said, indicating the flower piece.

''Oh, I'm pleased. That's a very good choice. It's a fine work by a contemporary British artist of some note. And though her name is not well known yet in the United States, I believe it will be in a very few years.'' Sybil spoke with enthusiastic assurance, and her eyes, which were deep-set and the color of strong coffee, were very alive and filled with a strong intelligence that was now alertly studying Kristi. ''You have an eye for excellence, you know.''

''Well, this painting really appeals to me, and I felt it had some quite exceptional qualities to it.'' She gave a brief shrug. ''And happily for me, it fell into my price range,'' she added, smiling.

''You know, since you're a friend of Chad's with an appreciation of good art, I'm hoping you will have better luck than I've had in convincing him to purchase some artwork of quality for his home. I'm sure you've seen that he's lacking in that area, haven't you?''

Kristi was amused at this ruse of Sybil's to discover how close a friend of Chad's she might be, and how familiar she might be with Chad's house. She gave Sybil a benign smile as she answered. "No, I'm afraid haven't been inside his half of the duplex."

Sybil's expressive face registered surprise first and then relief. "Oh for heaven's sake," she exclaimed, turning to Chad. "Why didn't you tell me Kristi was the cartoonist who's leased your duplex?"

"You didn't give me a chance," Chad said wryly. "With all this art talk you haven't even said hello to Mickey yet," he reminded her gently.

For the first time Sybil glanced down at the boy quietly standing close at Chad's side. "Gracious, Michael, I scarcely recognize you. You've grown taller since you were here last summer, and with your hair combed and your neat clothes, I must say you look quite grown-up and very nice."

A rosy flush appeared on his cheeks. "Thanks," he mumbled, looking down at his shoes so as not to look at her.

"I wasn't expecting to see you. Chad hadn't mentioned that you were coming. When did you get here?" There was an edge to her words and a frown flitted across her features.

"Yesterday," Mickey said, shuffling his feet, still not looking at her. It was obvious how uncomfortable Sybil's words made him feel.

"Yes, he arrived in all that rain," Kristi interjected. "Bless his heart, he even walked from the mall to Chad's and got pretty thoroughly soaked."

"Kristi saved the day, and Mickey and I are truly indebted to her. She found him on my back porch when she got home from work, took him in and got him into dry clothes, fed him supper, and kept him until I got in from Chicago about nine last night." Chad had turned to Kristi as he said this, and his warm smile echoed his words.

"My, that was an act of kindness, Kristi. I'm afraid I'm at such a loss around children. I wouldn't have a clue about how to entertain a boy Mickey's age for all that time. How on earth did you manage it?" Sybil threw out her hands, palms upward, in a gesture of helpless futility.

Kristi smiled and shrugged. "I assure you, it was easy. I simply fixed supper for a very hungry boy and let my little dog do the rest. You see, Mickey and Alex became well-acquainted during the long afternoon. They really hit it off. And you give a boy a pet to play with and both boy and dog are content."

"That's right. I remember that you have a dog. He's the one in your cartoon, Chad told me. I saw him in Chad's backyard one night last week."

Kristi gazed at the other woman in surprise, followed by curious interest. So Sybil Trevor was the lady she'd overheard in the backyard last Tuesday evening. This glamorous art dealer was the one who'd labeled dogs a nuisance and children a bother. However, her negative attitude didn't extend to Chad. She certainly found him quite to her liking. In fact, her manner toward Chad was proprietary, or at least it appeared that way to Kristi. And since Sybil apparently was pretty well acquainted with Mickey, talking about having seen him during his last summer's visit, that would indicate that Chad and Sybil's friendship was a long-standing one. Kristi found the idea of this oddly disturbing. For an instant she wondered why.

Realizing there was an awkward minute of silence between them, Kristi rushed to fill it. "Oh my, I'm sorry if Alex got in anybody's way. You must have seen him in the yard the day we moved in. There was lots of confusion for Alex with the movers going in and out and all. I expect he was curiously investigating all his new surroundings. I don't intend for Alex to bother or get in anybody's way. Actually, I've promised Chad that I'll be sure to keep my dog inside anytime he is entertaining guests outside. He can count on that from now on."

"That's very considerate of you, and of course it's truly necessary, since you and Chad share the porch and yard jointly." Sybil's voice was like silken oak. Too, there was a veiled challenge in her words that didn't escape Kristi. "Now, I really have to get back to the front of the gallery. So if you're ready, Kristi, come along and we'll take your new painting and get it wrapped for you to take home.'' Sybil managed her courteous, business smile as she lifted the floral picture off the wall. While her smile altered the firm set of her lips, it did not add the slightest bit of warmth to her eyes.

Chapter Five

Kristi walked cautiously out of the gallery, for the overall size of the framed painting she'd purchased made it awkward to handle and be able to see either around it or over the top of it. She had left her car at the back of the gallery parking lot, which meant she had to walk a short distance and also manuever her way among several rows of cars.

She had gone a few yards when she heard someone hailing her. "Hey Kristi, wait up and we'll help you!" Chad called out as he and Mickey sprinted to catch up with her. "I was going to offer to carry that for you back at the gallery, but I had to talk a minute with Sybil, and when I looked around, you had already gone," Chad explained as

50

he took the picture from her. "I like this thing, but it is a big son of a gun. I trust they don't charge you by the square inch for one of these," he said with wry humor.

"They don't." She laughed.

"Do you really think this will fit in the backseat of your car?" Chad asked as Kristi unlocked the door of her Taurus.

"Sure, I know it will."

"Well, frankly I have my doubts."

"Look, I saw a friend of mine put a painting bigger than this into a Volkswagen Bug once. So it can't be any big deal in a car like mine, which is taller and a heck of a lot roomier inside."

It took a bit of angling, but between Chad and Kristi they soon had the picture stowed away carefully across the backseat. "Well, you were right. The two of us got it in all right, but I don't think you can get it out by yourself. Promise me you'll wait for me to help you. If you wait until tomorrow, I could even help you hang it. We could do that before we make our trip to the mushroom farm. How about it?" Chad asked, cocking his head at her and giving her his most winning smile. "Will you let me show off my handyman skills at picture-hanging?"

"Sure thing. In fact, it would relieve my mind a lot for you to be hammering picture hooks into the walls of your duplex instead of me. I hung a few things myself today, but it was with fear and trembling.'' A suggestion of a smile touched her lips. ''So I guess we're still on for tomorrow. But if there's something you and Mickey would rather do, it's okay. We can go look at the mushrooms another time.''

''No way. Mickey and I talked to Greta on the phone last night. She and Eric are counting on us.''

''Yeah, Greta said she could hardly wait to see me,'' Mickey piped excitedly. ''She hasn't seen me since last summer and she's missed me lots. She says I'm her special boy,'' he declared rather proudly.

''Mickey spent six weeks with me last summer and Greta always came to sit with him when I had to be somewhere,'' Chad explained as Kristi got in her car. As he was closing the car door after her, he leaned his head down and lowered his voice. ''That was the first time Mickey had ever come for a visit alone. Catherine had always been with him before. It was a difficult time for all of us. Greta proved to be a godsend.''

''Catherine?'' There was a question mark in Kristi's voice. ''Is she Mickey's mother?''

''She was. She died a little over a year ago.'' His quiet voice was touched with sadness.

Kristi stared at Chad in bewilderment. This startling revelation left her totally confused. If Chad's wife was dead, why then wasn't Mickey living permanently with Chad? And who was the mysterious Jack? She'd figured out that Chad's wife, this Catherine, had probably remarried. But a step-father wouldn't have custody of a boy whose real father was living. It was obvious how much Chad cared about Mickey, and he certainly had the financial means to provide for him. Why then would his time with his son be limited to only a summer visit? Nothing about what she'd heard and seen would explain this arrangement now that she knew Mickey's mother was dead.

Chad had stepped back from the car, and Mickey was now standing beside him. So, though her mind was reeling with a dozen questions, she had no other option but to turn on the ignition and drive away.

As she drove back to Marlborough, Kristi couldn't stop conjecturing about the relationship of Chad, Catherine, and Mickey. At this point her curiosity knew no bounds. She made up her mind that she had to find an opportunity to talk to Chad when Mickey wasn't around. Chad had been so cautious about telling her what little he did in a quiet manner, so that Mickey wouldn't overhear, that it made it obvious Chad wished to shield the boy from any discussion of his mother's death.

Once again Kristi replayed through her mind exactly what Chad had told her. As she did, one new thing struck her as somewhat strange. Chad had said that last summer was the first time Mickey had come to stay with him without Catherine coming with him. That would indicate that even if he and his wife were divorced, they were on amiable terms, wouldn't it? Or maybe he and Catherine had not been divorced, just simply living apart for some reason. But that didn't explain this person named Jack. Where did he fit into all of this? Exactly how important a part did he play in Mickey's life? She found these thoughts distracting. Shaking her head and shrugging, she looked straight ahead, accelerated, and forced herself to concentrate now only on her driving.

On Sunday afternoon, the skies over the Philadelphia suburbs were cloudless and the deep blue color of hyacinths, making it ideal for a drive through the rolling countryside of the Brandywine Valley. Mickey was excited that Alex was going on this outing with them. Alex, too, seemed to sense that it was a special occasion for him. Always eager for a drive, the white and tan terrier wasted no time in climbing in the backseat with Mickey. He then sat up as tall as he could, pressed his nose to the window glass, and peered out to see the sights.

It was only a short drive from Marlborough to Kennett Square, and while Kristi tried to draw Mickey into conversation, he seemed happy and content to ride along without talking very much. In the brief two days since she'd discovered him on Chad's back porch, she'd found him to be a shy, rather quiet little boy. He was polite, of course, and would answer her questions with a word or two, but he seldom offered much information about himself on his own. She would discover that he was entirely different with Greta, however.

As Chad pulled the car into the drive at the side of the Muellers' white clapboard farmhouse, Mickey bolted out the car door and ran to meet Greta and Eric, who were waiting on the front porch. The minute he reached her outstretched arms, he began talking nonstop, and his high, bright voice rippled with laughter and squeals of joy.

Meeting this friendly German couple, she saw how accurate Chad's description of them had been. There were wings of gray in Greta's otherwise dark hair, and her violet-gray eyes held a gentle expression. As she talked with Mickey there was something soft and understanding in her face. She was drawing him out like a magnet, and listening to what he wanted to tell her with flattering absorption.

Greta and Mickey sat down together on the porch swing while Kristi and the men remained standing on the porch steps chatting. At her first opportunity, Kristi made a point of thanking Eric for hauling off all the packing boxes from her move.

"No problem, glad to do it," he assured her, a smile warming his weathered, angular face.

"You know what?" Chad said a minute or so later, placing his arm around Kristi's shoulders to claim her attention. "It's plain to see that Mickey and Greta have a lot of catching up to do. So I'm sure he won't miss us if we leave him behind and go cheek out the mushroom farm. How about it, Eric?"

"Fine, I'm ready anytime. We'll drive down in my truck. No need to get dust or gravel in that car of yours." He nodded his head in the direction of Chad's Buick.

Kristi quickly knelt down to fasten the leash to Alex's collar. "Will it be all right for my little dog to come with us? I'll make sure he doesn't bother anything."

"Ohhh sure," he drawled, a hint of his Pennsylvania Dutch heritage in his guttural voice. "Now, come along and let me show you how we go about producing these mushrooms of ours. I think you'll be surprised to discover that it's one of the most complex of all agricultural endeavors." He led them across the yard to where his blue and white truck was parked.

As they drove away from the house, Chad took

Alex from Kristi and held him on his lap. "I'll take care of the dog so you can give your full attention to Eric," he told her. "Eric, you need to explain all that stuff about the spawn to Kristi before we get down there. I remember you did that for me the first time I was out here, and I'm sure she's interested in knowing about everything that happens start to finish, aren't you Kristi?" He gave her a knowing wink. "You may not know it, Eric, but this gal is a cartoonist and an artist. She likes to use everything she sees in her work when she can. I promised her she'd gather a lot of ideas to use from learning about this mushroom wonderland of yours." As he said this, he gave her a conspiratorial look. "I also get a commission on what she draws from today's experience. So tell her lots of things to inspire her, Eric, won't you?"

Kristi gave Chad a wry glance. "You do go on, don't you?" She shrugged and turned her head toward Eric to hide the amused smile that traced her lips. "I do want to hear about how you grow mushrooms, though. Tell me, what is this spawn that Chad mentioned?"

"It's prepared material containing the rootlike mycelium of the mushroom, which is used to raise mushrooms commercially. This spawn germinates in incubators for four weeks and then is stored in cold storage until it's time to plant it." Eric paused, then looked at Kristi inquiringly. "Developing the spawn is a rather complex process, and done by skilled technicians. I'll try to explain the steps involved, if you'd like.''

"I probably wouldn't understand it if you did." She hunched her shoulders in a self-deprecating gesture. "I'm afraid I don't have a scientific mind, and as far as plant life goes, I can draw a flower, a leaf, a fern, or even a toadstool, but the biological science of mushroom cultivation is likely to escape me.''

"Well, I can't draw any of the things you can, so that makes us even," Eric countered, smiling at her. "Besides, we're coming up to the houses where we plant the spawn. I think you're going to find them quite interesting.''

As they approached several buildings, Eric stopped the truck and they all got out. Kristi gazed at the structure in front of her, a questioning frown on her face. "Didn't Eric refer to these as houses?" she asked, turning to Chad.

"Yeah. Look more like storage sheds, don't they?''

"Don't let the owners of these hear you call them sheds. They're very specially built windowless and air-conditioned houses," Eric was quick to say.

"But it's the fact that they don't have windows that makes it sound strange to call them houses." Kristi countered. '' 'Course, I didn't know they were air-conditioned. I guess mushrooms need a controlled environment. Right?"

Eric nodded. "That's right. You see, each one of these houses is lined on both sides by tiers of planting beds about six feet wide. When all the conditions are right, the spawn is spread on the beds and topped with a light covering of sterile soil. Then, approximately three weeks later, thousands of mushrooms appear and the picking process can begin." He paused and smiled at her. "I'm sure harvesting the mushrooms you'll find the most interesting part of the whole operation."

"Is that because it's what you do?"

"Well, actually, as supervisor I do some of everything, but the best part to me is putting on my miner's lamp and joining the other trained pickers."

Kristi looked bemused. "You wear those odd-looking caps with the light on the front?"

"Sure we do. We need them to light our way. Picking the mature mushrooms is a highly trained skill. We have to be able to distinguish mature mushrooms by shape and formation. You see, size actually has nothing to do with maturity. The pickers go over the bed every day for about two months, as the crop continues to mature and produce."

"That's fascinating. Did you know about the pickers wearing miner's lamps, Chad?" She turned

her head to draw Chad into the conversation.
"That part intrigues me."

"Way to go, Eric. You've got Kristi's artistic
wheels spinning now. I bet she's already picturing
Alexander with one of those lamps strapped to his
head sniffing out mushrooms in some dark, cave-
like place. Aren't you, Kristi?"

She flashed the two men an exuberant smile.
"You've got that right. I'm beginning to realize
that there are fabulous possibilities in all of this.
The mushroom is proving an amazing new phe-
nomenon to me."

"Actually, they are really an ancient delicacy in
a modern world," Eric stated matter-of-factly.

"How do you mean?" she asked.

"Well, the Egyptian hieroglyphics of four thou-
sand years ago recorded legends showing the
belief that the mushroom was the plant of immor-
tality. And the Japanese believed that one variety
of the mushroom could prolong life. The pharaohs
of Egypt were so intrigued with the delicious fla-
vor of mushrooms that they decreed that no com-
moner could ever touch one, thus assuring
themselves the entire supply. Furthermore, various
civilizations in Mexico, China, Siberia, Greece,
and Russia practiced mushroom rituals. Many believed that mushrooms contained properties which
would confer the ability to find lost objects, heal

the sick, produce supernatural strength, and aid the soul in reaching the realm of the gods.''

''That's glorious information. It blows my mind to think of all that I can do with it.'' Her voice escalated with excitement. ''Why, I can take Alexander the Small back in time to those ancient mushroom kingdoms. He can have more experiences than even Alice did in Wonderland. Eric, I can't thank you enough for telling me everything and giving me a real mushroom bonanza.'' Having said this, Kristi quickly put her arms around this kind man's neck and gave him a friendly hug.

''Hey, how about me?'' Chad immediately interjected. ''I'm the guy that brought you out here to view all this. It was my idea in the first place, you know.''

''Of course it was, and I'm mighty grateful to you too, Chad,'' she said, smiling sweetly and reaching up to pat his cheek affectionately.

''Then surely I deserve better than that,'' he declared, a roguish glint entering his compelling eyes as he took hold of her shoulders, lowering his face to meet hers.

The next moment, Kristi felt his lips touch hers like a whisper. Chad was only teasing and acting playful with her, she knew that. Yet the sweet tenderness of his kiss took her completely by surprise. Somehow, she sensed that it might have surprised him a little too.

Chapter Six

The sun was sinking low in the heavens when Kristi, Chad, and Mickey started driving back to Marlborough. Beautiful sunsets are a common sight in the Brandywine Valley. If the sky is clear, the horizon has all the shadings of a ripe peach. Creamy pink blends into rose and all shades of deep red. And when clouds mingle with the sunset, the colors are things only an artist dreams about. For clouds, dust particles, and crystal act as a prism to give us a new range of remarkable colors. Such was the view Kristi beheld, and she gave a deep sigh and said, "That's the most gorgeous sunset I believe I've ever seen. I'd give anything to have a painting that captured all those magnificent colors to hang on my living room wall."

"That reminds me," Chad said, sidling a look at her. "I promised to help you hang that new painting you bought yesterday. We'll do that first thing when we get back."

"And can I tell her what we're all going to do after that?" Mickey piped up from the backseat.

"Sure, it's your deal, Mick, you should be the one to ask Kristi and see if she's game to try it." There was a humorous undertone to Chad's reply.

"Game for what?" Kristi asked.

"A picnic out on the back porch. It was my idea," Mickey explained excitedly. "I went to the store with Chad and picked out the food and everything."

Chad chuckled. "See why I asked if you were brave enough to chance it? The menu is Mickey's choice, you understand."

Kristi looked over her shoulder at Mickey. "Well, I think it sounds like a special party, and I'm so glad you want me to come." She smiled at him and his eyes brightened with pleasure.

"I could tell you what we're going to have to eat, if you like."

It was obvious to see that the boy was eager to keep talking about this supper he'd planned. The fact that Kristi had called it a *special party* appeared to delight him, made him feel just a little bit grown-up and important. And of course what eight-year-old wouldn't enjoy basking in the attention of a kind, friendly lady, especially one who no longer has a mother to nurture and love him.

"I'd like that a lot," Kristi told him. "I think it's fun to anticipate all the cool things that you're going to get to eat. Don't you?"

Mickey bobbed his head. "Yeah, but it gets you hungry."

"Well, I'll need to be good and hungry at your picnic, 'cause I just know you picked out my favorite things."

He grinned. "Hot dogs, potato salad, and baked beans." His youthful voice had a questioning inflection in it.

"Absolutely top of my list," Kristi said, giving him her most engaging smile.

"Well, what do you know about that?" Chad shot a knowing look at Kristi and his eyes twinkled with warmth and humor. "And I'm betting that potato chips, pickels, and watermelon just happen to be on your list too."

"Yeah, how did you know?"

"Just a lucky guess." He gave Kristi a sly wink then before turning his attention back to the road.

True to his promise, a short time after they got back to the duplex, Chad came over to her side, a hammer in one hand and a yard stick in the other. "I took time to get the charcoaler set to grill our hot dogs before I came, and Mickey is going to get the table fixed and everything organized for us while you and I hang the painting.''

''Sounds like a masterminded plan, captain and crew busy each with a special job to do. You run a tight ship, sir,'' she said, saluting him and laughing.

''Actually, Mickey's running the show tonight. Like I told you, this is his party, and I really want to thank you for going along with the picnic idea like you did. You were great with him.''

''I wasn't just going along. I meant it. I'm a picnic-loving, summertime girl. Always have been.''

''You're a darn good sport too,'' he said, gazing at her, his remarkable eyes humorous and tender. ''You know, with Greta's and your help, we'll make this a good and happy time for Mickey while he's here.''

Curious as to the role Chad's friend Sybil Trevor played in Chad's life when Mickey was around, Kristi said, ''And your friend from the art gallery apparently knows Mickey. I bet she'll help you too.'' She managed to feign an innocent smile. ''Don't you think so?''

Chad frowned, his eyes level under drawn brows. ''Sybil is a busy lady, very involved with her gallery and other artistic and cultural pursuits. I'm afraid the places and things a boy Mickey's age enjoys are a bit too plebeian for her.'' He shrugged, his lips twisting into a cynical smile. Then, before Kristi could say anything more on this subject, Chad handed her the yardstick he was carrying. "Come on. We'd better get started hanging that picture of yours. Point out the wall where you want it and we can measure to determine the proper distance down from the ceiling or however you want to figure it. Someone told me once that a painting is hung so it's at eye level." He grimaced as he stated this. "Course, what I don't know is whether it's eye level for a five-foot-six-inch gal like you, or a six-foot-one-inch guy like me."

"I'm going to make it easy for you, because I've eyeballed the area where I want it and here's what you need to do. I want it hung centered over my long sofa there." She pointed to the very attractive, champagne-colored divan that spanned the focal wall of the living room. "I want the picture centered over my sofa and hung so the bottom of the frame is nine inches above the back of it. That'll be easy, won't it?"

"Piece of cake," he assured her. "Now you hold the painting while I take a few measurements. Then, after I make a couple of little pencil marks on the wall to go by, I'll hold it up in place for you to check it out. After that, I'll hammer the hook in the wall and we'll have the job done."

Kristi kept quiet while Chad was concentrating on his measurements, but when he picked up his hammer she went back to their earlier conversation.

"Chad, while we're talking about Mickey's visit here with you, there is something I'm mystified about. Would you mind if I asked you a personal question?"

"No, I don't think so," he said, continuing to hammer in the picture hook before turning around to look at her. "Go ahead, what is it?"

"Well, it's none of my business really, so don't answer if you'd rather not. But you told me that Mickey's mother was dead, so now I'm wondering why he doesn't live with you all the time."

Chad stared at Kristi, a totally confused expression on his face. "Because he lives with his father, of course."

Kristi's jaw dropped. "But you're his—I mean—I just naturally thought that you were his father," she stammered, her face growing red.

He shook his head, continuing to scrutinize her curiously. "Catherine was my only sister, and that makes me Mickey's uncle. I thought Mickey would have told you that."

"No, he didn't talk about his family. And I didn't ask because he was here on your porch, and he said he visited every summer. So I took it for granted that he was your son, and that you and his mother were divorced, so he lived with her somewhere and spent time in the summer with you."

"And obviously Mickey didn't tell you his last name was Wyatt."

"No, he told me his name was Michael but he liked Mickey better. And I told him my name was Kristine, but I liked Kristi better. That was the name exchange for both of us. I just let it go at that." She threw out her hands in a disparaging gesture. "I drew a lot of conclusions without getting any of the facts, didn't I?"

"Well, I can see how everything looked to you, and no wonder you were confused. But don't worry about it, and when we have more time, I'll fill you in about Mickey's parents. Right now, however, there's a little eager beaver waiting next door to get his picnic going, and you and I are not going to hold him up a minute longer." Chad grabbed Kristi's hand as he said this and propelled her rapidly in the direction of the back porch.

Kristi had to admit that she felt a sense of relief learning that Chad was Mickey's uncle and not his father. It was good that this nice, likable young boy had been spared the emotional upheaval of being shuffled back and forth between divorced parents. Also, she was glad to know that Chad didn't have a failed marriage in his past. She wasn't exactly sure why this seemed important to her, but it was.

A lot of questions had been raised in Kristi's mind now. She was curious about Mickey's mother, and what had happened to her. Presumably Catherine Coleman was within two or three years of Chad's age, younger or older. This meant she was only in her thirties when she died. And Mickey's father, what sort of man could he be? Hardly the fatherly type, if sending his son off with a truck driver and not even telling anyone to be on the lookout for him was an example of how he took care of his child. She ceased her conjecturing in time to give Mickey a helping hand serving up potato salad. For his gala picnic was now in full swing.

Some time after nine o'clock, a sleepy but happy Mickey went inside to put on a new pair of blue pajamas, and came back to the porch to give his uncle a hug and to shyly kiss Kristi goodnight before he headed off to bed. Chad went in to make sure the front of the house was secure, and to turn on enough lights to bathe the living room in a soft glow.

Meanwhile, Kristi wrapped what remained of the watermelon with plastic wrap and stored it in the refrigerator. She had just begun to load the dishwasher when Chad came back into the kitchen.

"I'll help you do that," he said, taking a handful of silverware out of her hand. "And then what do you say to a cup of cappuccino? We can sit and relax in my living room, which is like yours, except as Sybil informed you, my walls are lacking in all forms of quality artwork.'' Recalling Sybil's remarks, they both laughed.

At that moment, the wall phone in the kitchen rang sharply. Chad reached for the receiver. ''Hello,'' he answered. As he heard the voice on the other end of the line, a swift shadow of anger swept across his face. ''Yes, Mickey got here all right, if you call being let out to walk almost a mile in the pouring rain to get to my place all right. Not to mention waiting eight hours for someone to come home and find him. Why in blue blazes didn't you let me know he was coming? I swear, Jack, how can you act so irresponsibly with Mickey?'' Chad's voice was quiet, yet held an undertone of cold contempt.

Whatever this Jack responded, Kristi could tell it didn't appease Chad any. The phone was only two steps away from where she stood, continuing to load the dishwasher. Chad was facing her as he talked, so she not only heard every word of his side of the conversation, but caught every nuance of emotion that marked his expressive face. He appeared to listen to the other man for several seconds, a troubled frown narrowing his eyes. ''How long are you talking about, Jack?'' Chad's frown deepened. ''Well certainly I'll take care of him. But Mickey's not going to understand this. What do you expect me to tell him?''

As Chad listened to a lengthy answer to this question, he shook his head, appearing to be perplexed by what he was being told. "That's a strange thing for you to want me to do. Why would you think it was necessary?"

Suddenly Chad's puzzled expression changed to alarm. "What do you mean, *for his protection*? Listen here! You tell me exactly what this is all about right now," Chad demanded, his whole demeanor growing in severity.

A split second later Chad took the receiver away from his ear. "He hung up. Can you believe that? The guy throws a bombshell at me and without a word of explanation simply cuts out."

"That was Mickey's father, I take it." Kristi's eyes flashed with interest.

"Yeah, Jack Wyatt. Seems he finally got around to checking in to see if Mickey had gotten here. He also wanted to ask me to take care of him for a lengthy spell."

"You know, Mickey told me that first day that he was going to have a longer visit here this time than he'd had before. Did his dad say how long he wanted Mickey to stay?"

"He intimated that it could possibly be for a year. Seems he has some problems and a number of things have come up that he needs to take care of. Things he can't handle and look after Mickey at the same time, which doesn't surprise me.'' His voice had a caustic edge.

She looked at him curiously. ''What makes you say that?''

''Because Jack's never had time for much of anything but his music. He plays the piano and the guitar and sings a little. That's what he does for a living. He entertains in supper clubs, works with rock bands, plays backup for recording artists once in a while. If you entertain in a club, you work at night of course. What kind of care do you think Mickey gets when his dad works most of the night and his mother is dead?'' Chad said, his lips parting into a thin, grim line as he stood tall and solemn in front of Kristi. ''I've been concerned about this ever since Catherine died. And I know she trusted me to be there for Mickey, and I intend to be, but I just wonder how Mickey will take to being away from Jack for as long as a year.''

''Look, my bet is that you don't need to worry about that, certainly not this soon, at any rate. You know that Mickey fully expects to be here for an indefinite time. He's indicated that to me and you, and I think he told Greta that today too. And there's always the chance that Jack will get whatever problems he has solved in a shorter period than a year.'' She was trying to tell him everything reassuring she could think of. ''Besides, his father will be in touch with him, call and talk to him and send him presents and things, maybe even come here to see him,'' she added as an afterthought.

''I'm not so sure about that,'' he told her glumly. ''Jack made a strange request. One that worries me a lot.''

''What was it?''

''He said he wanted me to drop the Wyatt from Mickey's name.''

''Drop it—you mean not use it?'' She sounded as puzzled as she looked.

''Right. You see his full name is Michael Coleman Wyatt. Jack insists that he should now be known only as Mickey Coleman.''

''For heaven's sake why?''

''Jack claims it's for Mickey's protection.''

''Protection from what? From whom? I don't understand.''

''I don't understand it either. When I asked Jack to explain, that's when he hung up.'' Chad's face clouded with uneasiness. ''There's something strange about all of this. Jack has got to level with me and tell me exactly what's going on, and it darn well better not endanger Mickey in even the slightest way.'' Chad's voice was taut with anger and his brows were drawn down in a dangerous frown. He ran a frustrated hand through his hair, then exhaled. ''It's futile for me to worry about this anymore tonight,'' he said, looking at Kristi in his direct, serious way. ''I know of lots of nicer things you and I could talk about." He laid a hand lightly on her shoulder, appraising her with more than mild interest. "I bet you do too," he said, easing into a smile.

"You mean like mushroom cultivation?" Her voice was light and teasing.

"I mean like cultivating Kristi Saunders," he countered. "I'm interested in discovering all the interesting things about you that I haven't had time to learn yet."

Chad's words and manner caused a brief shiver to ripple through her as she became aware that there was an invisible web of attraction building between them. She felt a warmth flushing into her neck at the readable look of masculine appreciation in his eyes, and a tiny smile escaped into the corners of her mouth, dimpling her cheeks, as Chad raised his hand to push back a strand of her hair that had fallen across her face when she bent over to load the dishwasher. His fingers lingered for a moment in the silky strands before they slid caressingly across Kristi's cheek.

"I don't know what interesting things there are about me that you have yet to learn, but I'll try to think up some while you fix that cappuccino you promised me." Without looking away, she backed out of his reach, continuing to smile softly.

"You do that," he said, his eyes still bathing

her in admiration. There was something rather amorous in the look he gave her, but possibly Kristi didn't see it before she lowered her eyes and turned away.

Chapter Seven

In the weeks that followed, the mild June days came to an end and July ushered in deep summer air that was milky and breathlessly warm. During this time, and without being aware of just how it happened, Kristi was drawn into the pattern of Chad and Mickey's days.

When she thought about how involved she'd become, she felt that it was Mickey who had instigated most of it, although she wanted to believe that Chad wanted her to be a part of things as much as Mickey did. She sensed, of course, why Mickey had taken such a liking to her. From that first afternoon, when she'd found him in the rain and taken a genuine interest in him, Mickey felt he'd found himself a friend in Kristi. Then as the weeks passed she'd provided the gentle female touch, the soft caring voice and the interested listening ear, all things which were missing from his life since his mother's death.

On the day after the three of them had gone to the mushroom farm, Chad enrolled Mickey in a *summer day camp*. Chad took him on his way to work each weekday morning and picked him up on his way home in the late afternoon. It was a perfect arrangement and Mickey loved it. He received instruction in swimming and diving, and got to swim every day. Also the program included team sports, track relays, gymnastics, various handcrafts, and one field trip or outside event each week. When Mickey got home every evening he could hardly wait to run over to give Kristi a blow-by-blow account of each day's happenings. And at the end of the first two weeks he proudly presented Chad with a tooled leather bookmark, and Kristi with a small ceramic dog which he'd painted and fired.

"I know he doesn't look much like Alex, but it was the only sort of dog they had. I did try to paint him the colors of Alex, though."

"And you truly did," Kristi exclaimed with a show of genuine delight. "You have the light tan color on his ears and back, the creamy white on his face and legs, and you've even got the bit of darker brown in his tail." She gave him a bear hug. "You know, I believe you have an artist's eye for detail."

Kristi's words of praise brought a grin like three dollars worth of popcorn to Mickey's happy face. . . .

A week later, on a Wednesday morning, Kristi got a telephone call at work that took her completely by surprise. The only man who called her at the office was Derek Dryden, who was the brother of Becky, one of the other artists at Word Wise. Becky had arranged for Kristi to meet her brother several weeks ago, and since then they'd gone out together a few times. So when she heard a man's voice on the phone, she expected it to be Derek calling to set something up with her for later that week.

"Kristi, it's Chad," were the words she heard from the caller, however.

"Chad?" There was a question mark in her voice as well as an inflection that mirrored her surprise.

"Yeah, Chad, your next-door neighbor, and the older of your two devoted and ever-present boy-friends," he quipped.

She laughed. "I've never talked to you on the phone before. I just didn't expect it to be you."

"Well, it is me," he said, laughing back at her. "And I know it's pretty short notice, but I'm hoping you can get away today at noon and have lunch with me. I want to talk to you when it's just the two of us. I don't seem to have much luck sequestering you away from that very young and very devoted swain of yours, namely my nephew.'' He gave a verbal shrug. ''I want to talk to you about the little I've been able to find out about Jack. It's not too good, and of course I can't talk about it in front of Mickey. You can understand why.''

''Sure.'' She hesitated for a moment before adding, ''I guess I can do lunch okay—and noon will be fine. Shall I meet you somewhere?''

''No, I'll pick you up, that'll be easier. There's a place I like to go that's not too far from your building. Has good food, and they have always given me excellent service. So I can get you back to work whenever you say.''

''Sounds good to me. I'll be out in front, waiting for you to pick me up right at twelve.''

Kristi hung up the phone, but she didn't return to her work right away. She was anxious to find out just how much Chad had learned, and if he now knew the reason behind Jack wanting him to care for Mickey for as long as a year. Just the fact that Chad wanted to discuss it with her was exciting in a way. Certainly it pleased her that he chose to confide in her rather than in Sybil. Maybe Chad's relationship with Sybil Trevor wasn't as close as she had imagined. Thinking about that, she realized that to her knowledge Sybil had only come to the house once since Mickey had arrived. However, Mickey had told her that Greta usually stayed late on Thursday nights with him, because Chad went to Philadelphia to business meetings, dinners, shows, and grown-up things, was the way he put it. Though he never mentioned Sybil's name, Kristi figured the intriguing art dealer was one of the grown-up things.

The restaurant where Chad took her for lunch had a Country French decor as inviting as a stroll through a French vineyard. Almost the minute they arrived they were seated at a small round table with a unique base and an antiqued appearance, and the provincial-style chairs were designed with backs of small wooden spindles gathered to resemble sheaves of wheat.

"I can't wait to hear about Mickey's father. When did you talk to him again?" she asked as soon as their waiter had taken their order.

"I didn't. So far I haven't been able to locate him."

"But you've learned something about him." She angled her head toward him questioningly. "That's why you asked me to go to lunch, isn't it?"

"That was one of my reasons. Another one was

that I knew it would make my day to sit across the table from a beautiful lady cartoonist and eat the best French food in the Philadelphia area,'' he said, looking closely at her, his eyes bright with merriment.

''That's a charming thing to say, and I shall take it as a lovely compliment, even though I suspect I'm the only *lady* cartoonist that you know.'' There was laughter in her voice. ''However, the beautiful part is very flattering.''

''And very true,'' Chad said with quiet emphasis.

She exchanged a smile with him. ''Now, let's get back to Mickey's dad.''

He nodded his head. ''Okay, here's what I've done so far. First of all, I called the apartment where he and Mickey lived in Washington. I got that good old recorded bit—'the number you have dialed is no longer in service. If you think you have reached this number in error, please hang up and try your call again.' Well, I guess I should have anticipated that.'' He gave an offhand shrug.

''You think he's moved, or had his phone number changed?''

''Who knows? I did call information, too. They told me they had no listing for a Jack Wyatt anywhere in the Washington area. So my guess is he's either left town or wants everyone to believe he has.''

"Do you have any idea where he's been working?"

"I didn't, but fortunately Mickey knew the name of the club where he's been playing since just before the Christmas holidays last year. So I zeroed in on that as quick as I could."

Before Chad could tell her what he'd learned there, they were served their lunch. Their very attentive waiter hovered over them, serving everything with a continental flourish that he undoubtedly felt would earn him at least a twenty-percent gratuity. When he had made certain that he'd seen to their every need, he left them to enjoy what Kristi quickly discovered was superb French cuisine.

"So what did you find out at the supper club?" Kristi asked.

"Well, I had a curious conversation that may or may not shed some light on Jack's mysterious actions."

"That sounds encouraging. Tell me all about it." She inclined her head toward him, her eyes glinting with interest. "Who did you talk to—the club manager?"

"No. As a matter of fact I only talked to the guy who happened to answer the phone. Which might have been the best thing that could have happened. I think he gave me more information than I might have been able to get out of the manager.''

"How's that?''

"If I do say so myself, I handled it rather well.'' He tossed his head and gave her a cocky grin. "You see, I called just at the start of the dinner hour and asked for Jack.

"This fellow that answered the phone said, 'Jack who?'

" 'Jack Wyatt, the guy who plays piano there,' I told him.

" 'Not any more, he doesn't. He quit and I'm the piano man nowadays—Name's Marty Black.' That's what he tells me.

"Boy, this was a downer for me. So I quickly decided to act like I was a fellow musician, and I told him I was a good friend of Jack's and that he'd told me to be sure and look him up when I got to Washington. Said Jack had promised to help me get a job. This apparently piqued Marty's interest, because he asked me if I was a piano player like my friend Jack. I laughed, and said, 'No, I just strum a right fine guitar. But I sing as well or better than ol' Jack.'

"Now that this Marty and I had this good rapport going, I asked him if he could help me get in touch with Jack, and did he know if anyone there at the club could tell me where Jack had gone?'' Chad paused, leaned forward, and wagged his finger at Kristi. "Now listen to this. Here comes the interesting part. This fellow told me that when he was hired to entertain at the club, they told him that the fellow he was replacing quit because of family complications. But he went on to say that later on one of the waiters mentioned something about a shooting that took place right in front of the supper club about two months ago. Evidently the club got a lot of publicity because it appears Jack was the one who saw the whole thing happen. In fact, he was the one who gave the police a description of the killer. It seems it turned out to have been a gang-related homicide and Jack received threatening calls at the club, and when a note was left on the piano one night, the following day Jack quit, and no one saw him after that."

"Good grief, Chad, that sounds like the script of a Harrison Ford movie," Kristi exclaimed, frowning. "If that's really true, it's scary—terribly scary."

"I know it is," Chad agreed grimly. "By Jack making a positive identification of that killer, he set himself up as a target for gang retaliation, so not only is his life in danger, but Mickey's could be as well."

A wave of apprehension swept through her. "You can't let that happen, Chad," she said, in a tight, frightened voice. "There's got to be a way you can protect Mickey, and you've got to find it.''

"I've got a plan in mind, but I'll need your help to carry it out.'' His face was full of strength and there was a ring of determination in his voice. ''That's why I wanted to talk with you today. To ask you if you'd be willing to help me plan a scenario for a boy who is now *Michael Coleman*, and who may always be Michael Coleman if I have anything to say about it.'' He extended his hand, palm up. ''I need you in this with me, Kristi.'' There was a note of pleading in his voice.

After only a moment's hesitation, she put her hand in his. ''I'll help any way I can,'' she said gently.

He clasped his fingers around her hand as a quiver of emotion ran over his lean face. ''Somehow I just knew I could count on you.''

Chad's hand tightened, holding hers, and Kristi felt the warmth flowing between them. She experienced a rush of affection stealing into her heart for this compassionate man, and she suddenly realized how little it would take for that affection to turn into love.

Chapter Eight

Mickey's birthday was coming up on Saturday, and Chad had told Kristi that he was convinced that Mickey would hear something from his father by that time. "Jack Wyatt has his shortcomings, but he adored Catherine and he really loves Mick. He won't let his son's ninth birthday go by without a call or a present," Chad had said confidently. And it became very apparent that Mickey was as certain as Chad was that he was going to receive a package from Jack before the week was out.

"Did it come today?" Mickey called out to Greta on Thursday, the second he got home from day camp.

"Not yet, but I'll bet you'll get it tomorrow," she assured him. "Now sit down at the kitchen table and tell me what kind of icing you want on the chocolate birthday cake I baked today. I was waiting till you got home so you could choose either chocolate or white frosting.''

''I think I'd like white this time.'' He gave her a toothy grin. ''What color candles?''

Greta looked uncertain. ''Kristi's picking those up for me on her way home. I don't know what color she'll choose.''

''I hope it's yellow. Yellow is my favorite color next to blue.''

''Did I hear someone mention blue?'' Kristi asked, walking into the kitchen with Chad. ''I came to deliver the candles and Chad said I should come view the cake.''

''I'm afraid it's not ready for a showing yet. I haven't put the frosting on yet,'' Greta said with a negative wag of her head. ''Mickey and I were just trying to guess what color candles you would bring.''

''Well I didn't get blue.'' Her tone was apologetic. ''I thought on a chocolate cake, yellow would be a nice, bright color. Here,'' she handed the small box of birthday candles to Mickey.

He gave her a beaming smile. ''Yellow is really the color I wanted most.''

During their discussion of the birthday candles, Chad had stood quietly in the kitchen doorway, his hands behind his back. ''I think what you want

88   *Frances Engle Wilson*

most, Mickey, is what Kristi handed me when she came in,'' Chad said now, bringing forth the brown-colored cardboard box he had been hiding behind his back. "She said this package for you was leaning against the door when she got home a few minutes ago. It's addressed to an M. Coleman, so I guess it's definitely for you."

A radiant smile splashed across Mickey's face, and in his excitement he wiggled all over like an exuberant puppy. "My present—it came!" he cried, his voice spiraling in jubilation, as he ran to Chad and grabbed the package out of his hands. "I can't wait until Saturday. I'm going to open it right now. Can I?" He didn't wait for anyone to answer before hunting to find a spot where he could get the wrapping tape loose and rip it from around the box.

"Since that package didn't come through the mail, I wonder if we can discover where it came from," Kristi asked Chad in a quiet voice.

He wagged his head. "I doubt it."

"The UPS truck passed me as I turned into our street. Maybe they have a record of their deliveries."

"That's possible, but there could be a lot of red tape to checking on it, I bet."

Mickey had the box open now and was taking out a yellow knit polo shirt and a pair of khaki shorts. "Man, are these ever neat duds. Dad promised he'd get me some new things when he got the last of our bills paid off,'' he said, his young face aglow with delight. ''And look at this great shirt!'' He held it up for Chad to see. ''Look, it's got one of those special things on the pocket like your golf shirts, Chad.''

''Yeah it does have a designer logo, all right.''

''That means it's top-of-the-line merchandise for an A-number-one son,'' Kristi announced with a smile. ''Your dad really went all out for your birthday.''

Mickey's eyes sparkled with happiness. ''He sure did. And you know what this is on the pocket? It's a kangaroo, isn't that cool?''

''A kangaroo, that's quite a unique animal. They're native to Australia. That's interesting, don't you agree, Kristi?'' Chad gave her a knowing look.

''Looks like Mickey got a birthday card too,'' Kristi said, indicating the white envelope in the bottom of the box.

''Yeah, Mick, open that and let's see what it says.''

Mickey quickly pulled a red and blue decorated card from the envelope which had HAPPY BIRTH-DAY, SON in red letters on the front. He opened it and looked inside. ''Dad's written something in here.'' Mickey paused long enough to read what it said.

"What does it say?" Chad asked.

"It's a poem—or something, I guess." He wrinkled his face, looking puzzled.

"Well, read it out loud to us, won't you? Maybe I can tell you what it is." Chad took a step toward Mickey, keen interest narrowing his eyes.

Mickey hunched his shoulders. "Okay," he muttered, "but it sounds goofy to me." He held the card up in front of him and read:

In faraway places,
A new-sounding name.
You follow the rules,
Or you can't play the game.

"Sounds like a riddle to me, doesn't it to you, Kristi?"

She nodded her head. "Sort of. We'll all need to put our heads together and see if we can figure it out."

Chad held out his hand. "Let me keep the card, Mick, and I'll study it and see what I can make of it. That's okay with you, isn't it?"

"Yeah, sure," he said, giving the card to Chad.

Greta had the white icing made by then, so Mickey's attention was again centered on his birthday cake. Kristi immediately made her exit out the door to the porch. This being Thursday, she felt it was most likely that Sybil was coming to Chad's for dinner, and she didn't want to go out the front door and risk running into Sybil as she was arriving. Greta always cooked a great meal when she was there on Thursdays. Kristi remembered that today the kitchen was filled with the appealing smell of the two layers of chocolate cake plus the appetizing odor of ham baking in the oven. This plus Greta's urgent need for a box of tiny candles indicated to Kristi that an unplanned, early celebration of Mickey's birthday had been quickly arranged in order to include Sybil.

Kristi continued to speculate on this as she went inside her own kitchen and set about preparing her dinner of broiled red snapper, green peas, a baked potato, and a tossed green salad. She knew that the real celebration for Mickey's birthday was to be on Saturday. A renowned circus had arrived in Philadelphia and Chad and Mickey had insisted that Kristi go to the Saturday afternoon performance with them. "It's my birthday party," Mickey had explained to her with enthusiasm. "And I want you to go to the circus with Chad and me."

She was Mickey's choice, and of course she was going with them. Yet she couldn't help but wonder if Sybil might have been Chad's choice. Perhaps he'd even asked her, and Sybil, who hardly seemed like the circus-going type, had turned him down and opted for bringing a birthday present and having dinner with Mickey and Chad tonight. She grimaced, then quickly chastised herself for allowing Sybil's proprietary attitudes concerning Chad to bother her. After all, Sybil obviously had figured in Chad's life for some time. He might even be in love with her. On the other hand, Kristi was just Chad's tenant, someone who lived next door, who had befriended the motherless boy that turned out to be Chad's nephew. It was Mickey who'd formed a loving attachment to Kristi. He was the one who wanted her to share in the things he and Chad did and the places that they went. It was like she'd thought. She was Mickey's choice, but Sybil was Chad's, and it behooved her to remember that fact.

When Saturday came, it was a radiant and balmy day that invited and beckoned. The morning sky was fresh, with blue sprays of feathery clouds. Sunlight filtered through the leafy domes of the trees. There was a gentle breeze and the leaves rustled and trembled under it, and shimmered with green brilliance as they caught the sun.

They drove into Philadelphia quite early in the afternoon because Mickey wanted to make sure they had time to see absolutely everything. People were milling about the crowded parking lot when they arrived, and circus performers in colorful costumes were mingling with the spectators. The July sun was bright overhead now, since it was just a little past midday. On the grounds, large striped tents had been set up to protect the cages housing the animals. Chad, Kristi, and Mickey joined the masses converging on the large arena, and nearing the elliptical-shaped building, they could hear the calliope music drifting through the open doors.

Inside, they were met with a pungent odor of sawdust and animals mixed with the aroma of fresh-roasted peanuts and popcorn.

"Let's get some cotton candy, then so see the animals," Mickey volunteered exuberantly.

"Good idea," Chad agreed. "The performance doesn't start for at least an hour."

They approached one of nearly a dozen concession stands, and then, cotton candy cones in hand, they headed for the animal tents. They strolled along the grassy, makeshift aisles between the rows of straw-bedded enclosures, petting the elephants tied outside, laughing at the costumed clowns who were already performing their antics for the children.

Kristi loved the entire atmosphere, and the vivid colors. Mickey barraged Chad with questions about the animals—where the circus got them and how they took care of them and transported them all from town to town. Kristi listened to them, awed by the number of question Mickey came up with, and equally amazed by Chad's colorful and sometimes imaginative answers. P. T. Barnum himself couldn't have done better.

Later, when they were in their grandstand seats, the show finally began. They had an excellent view of the three rings below. Chad sat between Kristi and Mickey and they all applauded enthusiastically at the opening parade and the ringmaster's introductions. Mickey sat on the edge of his seat clapping madly at the ensuing performances. Kristi shifted back from the edge of her seat and was only slightly less fervent.

When they started the high-wire acts, however, Kristi became anxious. She gazed up at the man slowly inching his way across an overhead cable that, from her vantage point, looked like nothing more than a gossamer filament. He held a balancing bar precariously in front of himself with both hands. Leaning over to Chad, she said in a stage whisper, "He scares me to death. I thought these guys worked with nets. I'm afraid to watch."

Chad took hold of her hand, squeezing her tense fingers reassuringly. "Don't worry. He's one of the great Garzanellis. They're the most famous aerialists in the world today."

"Even so, I can't look." There was a tremor in her voice. She bowed her head and closed her eyes.

Chad pulled her head into the hollow of his shoulder. "Just take it easy, baby," he said, resting his cheek against her soft brown hair. "The high-wire acts will be over soon, and then they'll bring in the clowns." His tone was gentle, but there was a sound in his voice that was somewhere between a caress and a tease.

When the circus was over, there was considerable traffic leaving Philadelphia, so it was close to six o'clock by the time they had driven back to Marlborough. As their car rounded the corner leading into their street, they noticed a dark green car was parked directly in front of the duplex.

"Before we get too close, see if you can tell where the license plate on that car comes from," Chad said, easing the car to a much slower speed. "I don't think it looks like a Pennsylvania tag."

"No, it's not," Mickey piped up. "I recognize it. It's District of Columbia." He sounded pleased with himself to be able to identify it so quickly.

Chad turned to Kristi, a grim expression lining his face. "That car worries me. I sure don't like it." He looked over his shoulder to Mickey. "Listen, Mick. Get down on the floor out of sight right this instant. I don't want whoever is in that car to see you. Now here is what we're going to do," he continued, as he accelerated, drove past the parked car, and wheeled quickly into his driveway. "I'm driving straight into the garage and don't move until the garage door is completely down behind us. Then I want us to go in the back door and get in the house as fast as we can. Mickey, you're to go into the back bedroom and stay there. Don't make any noise. If someone comes to our door, I want him to think that the only people here are Kristi and me.''

The three of them had scarcely gotten inside the house when the doorbell rang, followed by several sharp claps of the door knocker. With a silencing finger against his lips, Chad scooted Mickey into the back bedroom.

Then he took Kristi's hand and together they started into the front part of the house. ''I'll answer the door Kristi, and you stay behind me a little way where they can see there's a woman in the house. Go along with whatever I say and we'll play it by ear. It may be nothing at all, but we've both got to be careful.''

The doorbell sounded again and Chad let go of Kristi's hand and quickly walked to the front door and opened it. A stocky fellow casually dressed in khaki trousers and a khaki-colored short-sleeved shirt was standing there.

Kristi had positioned herself close behind and slightly to the side of Chad, where she could see the stranger clearly through the open door. He appeared to be somewhere around thirty, she thought. He was clean shaven, with medium-length dark hair. The thing that struck her most about him was his strange mud-colored eyes under an untidy hooked line of eyebrows.

"Can't tell you how glad I was to see you folks drive in just now," the young man said, extending his right hand to Chad. "My name is Nick Varley, and I'm hoping you're Chadford Coleman."

Chad nodded. "Yes I am."

"Good, that's a break for us. You see my friend out there?" he gestured with his thumb over his shoulder to indicate the car parked in front of the duplex. "The two of us have been waiting around here most of the afternoon to have an opportunity to talk to you, Coleman. It's necessary that we get in touch with Jack Wyatt and members of his family, and we understand he's a relative of yours." He quirked his eyebrow questioningly.

"Of sorts. I guess you could say he was." Chad feigned a look of disinterest and shrugged. "Jack was once married to someone in my family. But that was a while back. He and I never had much to do with each other."

"Is that right?" Nick's tone was disbelieving.

"Yeah," Chad said, thrusting his chin up at a confident angle and thrusting his hands in his pockets. "So I'm afraid I can't be of any help to you. I really haven't seen or heard much about him in the past couple of years."

"Well, maybe you could tell me something about his family. He's got a wife and kids, hasn't he?'' The stranger retained his affability, but there was a distinct hardening of his eyes. ''I'd appreciate even the smallest bit of information that you could give me.''

Chad eyed the other man thoughtfully and Kristi held her breath, wondering what Chad was going to tell him. ''Well, let's see,'' Chad said, easing his hands out of his pockets and then assuming a relaxed stance and folding his arms across his chest. ''I know his wife died a year or so ago. I think they had one or two children. I'm not sure, though. As I told you, I haven't kept up with Jack and his family.'' Chad paused, eyeing Varley questioningly. ''What's your big interest in Jack Wyatt?''

Nick shrugged. ''Just need to locate him, that's all. Figured he might be staying with a relative or maybe taking his kids on summer vacation.''

''Is he a friend of yours, then?''

''No, I don't know him,'' Nick answered with a negative shake of his head. ''An associate of mine must get in contact with Wyatt, so I'm checking out some folks, trying to turn up some leads for him.''

''Well, I guess I wasn't any help to you, but I simply have no idea at all where he might be. Furthermore, I can't think of a person who might be able to help you.'' Chad stepped back from the door as he said this, indicating that as far as he was concerned, their conversation was over.

Nick Varley obviously got Chad's message, for he muttered, "Thanks anyway." Then he turned on his heels and walked rapidly off the porch and back out to his car.

Chad immediately closed the front door and turned to Kristi. "Thank goodness that's over," he said, heaving a sigh of relief.

"Chad, you handled that fellow like a pro, and you appeared so calm and matter-of-fact. You were amazing."

"At least I did get rid of him in short order," he said, jamming his hands in his pockets rather defiantly.

"You also convinced him that you didn't know much of anything about Jack and his family. You're quite a good actor," Kristi said, giving him a pat on the back.

He thrust his chin up proudly. "I do think I pulled it off okay, at that."

"You certainly did. Really, you gave a stellar performance."

Chad laughed. "Just call me Jack Nicholson. . . ."

Chapter Nine

Kristi's steps were buoyant as she left work on Friday. Earlier that afternoon her boss, Luther Farmington, had called her into his office to tell her that he had approved not just one or two, but all six of her Alexander the Small birthday card designs. And he was equally enthusiastic about the four Alexander get well card designs she'd submitted most recently. On top of this, he'd told her to begin thinking about special occasion cards with her famous cartoon dog. He was interested in an Alexander valentine and something clever and original for Graduation Day particularly.

Now the image of Alexander wearing a mortarboard atop his shaggy head and carrying a diploma in his teeth kept her smiling as she drove home through the Friday afternoon traffic. When she arrived at the duplex, she came in through the front door so she could pick up her mail. There was nothing of real interest, so she laid it aside and walked to the glass doors at the back to check on Alex. She could see him stretched out asleep under the sun-shielding elm tree in the middle of the yard. It made a pleasant scene, for the late-afternoon sun was waning, and tossed its yellow shafts of light down into the break in the awning of the trees, painting the ground below in patterns of light and dark. She was about to open the door and call Alex in when the phone rang.

"Hello," she said brightly, moving the phone from the kitchen counter to the table so she could sit down and talk.

"Hello Kristi, it's Chad. I'm glad you drove straight home. I called you at work about forty minutes ago and they said you'd just left. I sure hope you don't already have plans for tonight, because it has suddenly turned out that this is the perfect time for us to do something really special—just the two of us."

"Hey, you're going too fast for me. What exactly are you talking about?"

"About you and me going out together to a great restaurant and having a romantic dinner with music and wine—only the two of us—because, you see, Greta and Eric have invited Mickey to

102 *Frances Engle Wilson*

spend the night at the farm with them, and then tomorrow they're taking him and their two grandsons to the Dutch Wonderland Fun Park over in Lancaster for the day.'' Chad offered the explanation in a run-on spiel, pausing finally to take a quick breath and add, ''Please tell me you're free tonight and that you'll let me take you to Nicolette's for dinner.''

Hearing the eager tone in Chad's voice sent a warm glow flowing through her. ''I'd love to go,'' Kristi said enthusiastically. ''It sounds wonderful and I'm glad you happened to think of me.''

''Oh, I just happen to think of you quite a lot,'' he said, with a low, throaty laugh.

As Kristi was showering and getting dressed, she thought about the several different places she'd eaten out with Chad and Mickey. Those times they had gone to pizza parlors, or to the popular chain restaurants for fried chicken or cheeseburgers, all casual-dress, family-oriented places where folks usually take their kids. Tonight, of course, was an entirely different story. For this was to be special, and Chad was taking her to an upscale, four-star restaurant renowned for its French Provençal cuisine and the gracious ambience of its Mediterranean-style setting.

Rising to the occasion of dining at Nicolette's, Kristi sensed, would require her to wear an outfit of understated elegance, feminine, yet not fussy, stylish yet not low-cut or obviously sexy. As she contemplated her adequate, but not extensive wardrobe, it came down to her essential, always suitable, *little black dress*. She took it out of the closet and looked at it. Though it was very chic, which would be right for a bistro or a club, somehow it wasn't the look she wanted for herself. It simply wasn't as romantic as she'd like to appear tonight with Chad.

It was at that moment that she suddenly thought of the silk sheath dress with the matching hip-length jacket that she'd bought in Baltimore last summer. It was the very thing. For it was that exquisite shade of soft red mixed with orange, the exact color of sea coral, and the simple lines of the dress showed off her slender, nicely proportioned figure while the lucious color looked great with her misty green eyes and her tawny brown hair.

When Chad came to pick her up, she knew she'd made the right choice, for he looked at her as if he were photographing her with his eyes. "Wow!" he said, as his gaze traveled over her. "You look terrific!"

She felt a ripple of excitement at his obvious examination and approval. "Thanks," she said, her cheeks coloring under the heat of his gaze. "You look pretty sharp yourself."

He leaned down and whispered in her ear, "That's good, because you see, there's this knock-out good-looking neighbor of mine who has mostly seen me with cotton candy on my face and barbecue sauce on my shirt. I've got to show her that I can clean up into a right presentable guy." He let his lips brush across the edge of her ear before he lifted his face.

"Oh, I think she's aware of that," Kristi said, her eyes smiling up into his. They shared a moment of intense physical awareness of each other, then Chad took her arm and they walked out to his car together.

As Kristi and Chad entered Nicolette's, a medium-size man with curly black hair touched with gray jumped up from one of the regal French benches and hurried across the foyer toward them.

"Chad, it's good to see you," he said in a warm, mellow voice that held just a trace of a Southern drawl. "Miriam and I were sitting over there waiting for our dinner guests to arrive, and I looked up and saw you come in. You must come over and say hello to Miriam and introduce this lovely woman to us." His rather boldly handsome face smiled warmly down at Kristi as he said this, and there were age lines about his mouth and eyes that gave him that distinguished senatorial look.

"My name is Ed Braxton, by the way," he added, taking her arm.

The three of them approached Ed's wife, and Chad introduced Kristi to Miriam Braxton, who was an attractive woman in her early fifties with auburn hair, a well-modeled face, and a look of loving to pamper herself. She acknowledged Kristi with an appraising look and a smile. And though her lips were parted, her eyes were somber, refusing to echo the smile.

"I think I've heard your name before, Kristi. I believe you're the artist Sybil mentioned who's living in Chad's duplex."

"Miriam is Sybil's mother, and Ed's her stepfather," Chad explained quickly.

Kristi smiled as she searched for something gracious and appropriate she might say. "I met Sybil at her gallery a few weeks ago. My, she offers many marvelous works. I found the perfect flower painting for me, and Sybil told me some interesting background on the artist. She had this information right at her fingertips. It's easy to understand why she's making a great success with the Trevor Gallery."

"She's a go-getter all right," Ed attested heartily.

"Of course, Sybil is very thorough in whatever she does, and she does it well," Miriam said, arching her neck proudly. "I will say that when she wants something, she doesn't let anything or any-body stop her from achieving her goal.''

Kristi couldn't help but feel the innuendo in Miriam's words. She stole a glance at Chad to catch his reaction. His expression was noncom-mittal, but he did immediately put his hand on her arm. ''Our reservation is for eight o'clock. We'd best go,'' he said quickly. ''Really nice to run into you two,'' he added, giving the Braxtons a fare-well nod as he led Kristi away.

There was the look of summer in the dining area of Nicolette's. The tables were covered with pastel-green cloths with petal pink overlays. Each table was centered with a small crystal bowl which held a nosegay of summer flowers, and the tables were set with crystal goblets, sparkling wine-glasses, and glistening silverware. Melodic music floated through the room, forming an enjoyable background of sound without intruding on the din-ers' conversations.

It wasn't until after they had ordered and their waiter had taken away the large impressive menus that Kristi broached the subject of Sybil's parents.

''It was nice that you ran into the Braxtons. I take it you've known Sybil's folks for quite a long time.'' She tried to make it sound like she was just making a casual observation and a bit of idle conversation.

''Not really.'' He gave a negative shake of his

head. "Ed is the one I've know for several years. He's an engineer with DuPont, and we got acquainted first in a business way. His first wife was still living at that time."

"Did you know her?"

"Yeah, they asked me to a Christmas party at their house in Wilmington two years in a row. She was a lot like Ed, very sociable and friendly. They made a great couple. Sure was sad that she died. I think she was only in her forties."

"What happened?"

"I don't know exactly." He shrugged. "She had to have some kind of surgery, and there were some unexpected complications. She never came out of the anesthesia."

Kristi sighed. "That's tragic."

"It sure was hard on Ed. He had a mighty lonely time of it for several years. Then, about eighteen months ago, he met Miriam. They seemed to click right off, and it was at their wedding last year that I met Miriam and, of course, Sybil."

Kristi looked puzzled. "I thought, since Sybil seemed to know Mickey fairly well, that she was a longtime friend of yours."

"She met Mickey last summer when he spent some time with me while Jack had a job entertaining on one of those Caribbean cruise lines."

At this moment they stopped talking, because their waiter served an intriguing-looking salad of curly-leaved chicory and chopped walnuts with a creamy Roquefort cheese and lemon dressing. This French salad was garnished with nasturtium flowers which the waiter assured them were not only for decoration but had a delicate peppery taste.

Once they began to eat, Kristi figured she'd learned all she was going to about Sybil and her family from Chad. Even though she was curious about Sybil and Chad's relationship, she wasn't going to make it obvious by questioning him further.

"Who'd have ever thought that Roquefort cheese and walnuts could taste this delicious?" she commented when she'd eaten several bites.

"It is good," Chad agreed. "And unusual. But that's why people come to Nicolette's, because it's an adventure in great eating."

"*Vive l'aventure*—and *vive la Nicolette*," she said, laughing.

"Look Kristi, I think I should explain something else about Sybil, so you'll understand where she's coming from." Chad's voice became serious.

Kristi sucked in her breath in surprise. All of a sudden she wasn't too certain that she wanted to hear more about Sybil after all. This was a special evening for her and she wanted to keep it that way. She crossed her fingers and tucked her hands down in her lap, hoping against hope that Chad was not going to tell her something that would spoil this perfect night for her. "You don't need to tell me anything else. I was only interested in learning about your friend Ed and Sybil's mother mostly. They seemed like a nice couple and quite good friends of yours," she rattled on in a rush of words. Then, realizing how foolish she must have sounded, she stopped.

"I really think you should know this, Kristi. It will help explain some things about Sybil. You see, Sybil is an only child, so she never had to share with anyone, or vie with a brother or sister for her parents' love or attention." Chad spoke in an odd, yet gentle tone. "Her father died when she was in her teens. Then it was just Sybil and her mother for all those years, until Ed came on the scene. Now suddenly she was no longer her mother's sole interest. I think it's been very difficult for her to come to terms with this. She's really rather an insecure person," he added with quiet emphasis.

"To meet her, you'd think she was exactly the opposite. Why at the gallery that day she appeared so self-assured and assertive." Kristi frowned thoughtfully. "I took her to be a take-charge, highly competent, successful businesswoman."

"Well, she is all those things, but that doesn't change the fact that she feels threatened if someone takes any attention away from her—even if it's only a child."

Kristi stared at Chad. "Are you saying she resents your having Mickey here with you?" Her voice spiraled questioningly.

"Let's just say she finds it inconvenient. An active nine-year-old interferes with Sybil's summer agenda," he said drily. "And Mickey senses this, of course."

It disturbed Kristi to hear this, and she couldn't help but wonder why Chad would be revealing so much about Sybil to her. "Look, Chad, I—I scarcely know Sybil," she stammered. "I honestly don't understand why you'd be discussing her with me."

His square jaw tensed visibly. "I realize that, Kristi." He held his hand out in a silencing gesture. "But just hear me out, and you'll understand. You see, a few nights ago, I was talking to Mickey about his going to school here this fall. When I said this he looked kinda funny and said, 'I wasn't sure you wanted me to stay here with you and go to school.' "

"I wonder what made him think that?"

"That's what I asked him. Guess what his answer was?"

Kristi shook her head. "I can't imagine."

"Well, he said that he knew Sybil didn't like him, and didn't really want him staying here for a long time."

"Oh, my word, Chad. That's pitiful. What on earth were you able to say?"

"I tried to make light of it," Chad said with a shrug. "I told him not to worry about Sybil, that she wasn't accustomed to kids, and she just didn't understand how to talk to them or do things with them. I passed it off as best I could. That was about all I could do." His expression was grim as he spoke, and his eyes were hooded like a hawk. "And I assured him that I wanted him here, and that was what counted."

"He accepted that okay, didn't he?" Kristi asked, a note of concern in her voice.

"Well, I thought he did at first. But later he looked really unhappy, and it was then that he said something that I think you'll find as upsetting as I do."

She looked at Chad in alarm. "What do you mean? What did Mickey say? Tell me."

Chad pushed his salad plate aside, resting his right hand on the edge of the table as he leaned forward to answer her. "Mickey said that he wouldn't want to stay here for a whole year and go to school if I thought it would bother you to have him hanging around all that time. Because then you might not like him anymore."

"Oh no! How could he even think such a thing? Poor little guy." Her voice echoed the distress mirrored on her face. "Chad, we've got to do something right now so Mickey will understand how much I like seeing him every day, hearing about the things he's doing. And nothing is going to change my affection for him. You tell him that when he comes home from Greta and Eric's. Tell him that we became friends in the rain, and rainy day friends are the best kind, because they stick together rain or shine.''

"I'll tell him exactly that," Chad said, a satisfied light coming into his eyes. "I believe you understand now why I felt I should tell you about Sybil. Though she didn't do it intentionally, she upset Mickey. Now he's unhappy and worried, thinking both you and I may reject him too. The good part is that I can count on you to help me reassure Mickey that we want him to stay, that he belongs here for this year and for just as long as it takes Jack to be in a position to take care of him again." He paused, his face creasing into a sudden smile. "And about this *rainy day friend* thing of yours. I want to be one of those. Actually, I'd say I already qualify."

She cocked her head. "How so?" she asked, sounding amused but skeptical.

His earnest eyes sought hers. "Because it rained the day we met," he said, emphasizing his words with authority.

"You're making that up," she scoffed, frowning at him. "I don't remember any rain that afternoon. I drove from Philadelphia to Marlborough and the highway wasn't wet. There may have been clouds in the sky, but I certainly didn't have to use my windshield wipers because of any summer shower. So what kind of hoax are you trying to play on me?'' She gave Chad an amused look, then picked up her fork to take the last few bites of her salad.

"Look, I didn't say it was raining at the exact time that we met. It had rained earlier that day however, and that makes it qualify as a rainy day. Think about this for a minute.'' He held up his index finger and shook it at her to get her attention. "After you'd looked all around the rooms inside, we went outside on the porch so you could check out the yard. You surely recall our conversation about my expertise with the charcoal broiler on the one hand, and Alex's delight at having a yard to roam around in on the other.''

Kristi's lips quirked with humor. "Of course I do. You thought Alex was my husband, and I thought you weren't going to let me have the duplex when you discovered Alex was a dog.'' She chuckled at the memory.

"Okay then. Now that I've reminded you about being outside, maybe you'll recall that we didn't leave the porch to walk around in the yard because the ground was still damp from the rain, and there were even puddles of water at the base of the porch steps.''

Kristi pursed her lips thoughtfully, a bemused look crinkling the corners of her eyes. ''You know, I do remember how lush and green everything looked. I guess you're right. It probably had rained that day in the suburbs, it just didn't rain all the way into Philadelphia.''

''My point exactly. I rest my case.''

Chad's pleasant chuckle reverberated through her as they exchanged a look of amusement. ''I think we've just had one of those Shakespearean conversations—much ado about nothing,'' she told him, teasing laughter glinting in her eyes.

''You're quite wrong, Kristi. It was far from being about nothing.'' Suddenly all the laughter was gone from Chad's eyes. He looked at Kristi, his gaze as soft as a caress. ''When two people are discovering a tangible bond between them, believe me, that is *something*.''

There was now a deeper significance in their visual interchange. And at the base of Kristi's throat she could feel a pulse beat and swell as though her heart had risen from its usual place.

They lapsed into silence as their salad plates were removed and they were served their main dish, Poulet Niçoise, which was a specialty of the house. This chicken sautéd with a wine sauce was garnished with quarters of artichokes, baby zucchini squash, small new potatoes, and black olives coated with the wine sauce and sprinkled with tarragon. As she and Chad enjoyed the superb French cuisine, they talked only of light, inconsequential things, yet the undeniable magnetism that they both felt remained there between them.

It was the dark hour of the night when they left the restaurant. Chad put his arm around Kristi's shoulders and held her close to him in the curve of his arm as they walked the short distance to his car. Outside, the summer night air was fragrant, and clusters of small stars shone high above. As they headed out toward Marlborough, the lights of Philadelphia floated like fireworks in the darkness.

"Thanks for a wonderful evening, Chad," Kristi said as they stood together in front of her door. "I enjoyed every second of it."

"Me too," he said, his compelling eyes gazing into hers in expectation.

Kristi moved toward him slightly, or seemed to move, and he quickly swept her into his arms. He held her gently at first, then pressed her hard against him. "I think you and I are going to be more than just rainy day friends," he said huskily. "What do you think?"

Her answer was unspoken. She simply turned her face up to his. A sensuous light passed between them as Chad lowered his face and pressed his lips against hers, then gently covered her mouth. His kiss sang through her veins, causing an unsteady beat of her heart and an inner trembling that had nothing to do with weakness—rather it was evidence of the momentous effect of his kiss.

When it ended, she stepped out of the circle of his arms and quickly unlocked her front door. As she walked inside, she turned slightly to look back at him. "Good night, Chad," she murmured.

"Good night, Angel," he said. His voice was husky and low, and Kristi wanted to believe that his words were an expression of endearment.

Chapter Ten

Despite the fact that Kristi hadn't gotten to bed until well after midnight, she didn't get to sleep in on Saturday. Alex saw to that. This dog of hers had a built-in alarm system that went off every morning at seven o'clock. Saturday, Sunday, or holidays were no exception. His blue and green plaid cushioned dog bed was at one end of the hall near Kristi's bedroom. If she wasn't already awake and up by seven, Alex would pad quietly into her room, put his front paws up on her pillow, and make little whimpering sounds in her ear until she opened her eyes and spoke to him.

"Alex, don't you know it's Saturday and I was out very late last night?" she grumbled, as she walked barefoot to the kitchen door to let him out into the backyard. "Now go play and don't bark or disturb our neighbor," she cautioned, giving him a beef juice–basted, rawhide bone. "Chew on this and let me grab another hour's sleep." Alex took the bone in his teeth and trotted off obediently as if he understood every word she'd said and was happy to accede to her wishes. "Good boy, Alex," she said, turning immediately and heading back to her bed.

Ding . . . ding . . . Two sharp rings of the door-bell, followed by a vigorous succession of knock-ing startled Kristi into wakefulness again. She thought she'd only been back asleep a few minutes, but as she grabbed up her robe she saw that the Waterford crystal clock on her dresser said fifteen minutes before nine.

A series of staccato rings came again. "Hey, I'm coming," she yelled, scooting into the entry hall. She cracked the door open, leaving the chain on until she could see who it was.

"I have a special overnight mail delivery for Chad Coleman," the young uniform-clad delivery man announced. "I need you to sign for it."

Kristi shook her head. "Coleman is that other door. This is a duplex."

"I know," he nodded. "I tried that side, but got no answer." He frowned, and pushed his billed cap back off his forehead, appearing frustrated. "This is guaranteed next-day delivery, you see. I'd sure appreciate it if you could help out and sign for it. I've already put a notice on Coleman's door that I've left this with you.'' He indicated a large envelope.

Kristi shrugged and opened the door. ''Okay, sure. I can do that.''

He held out his clipboard. ''Just sign there on line number three,'' he said, giving her a pen, and pointing to the proper place.

''I imagine he'll be at home later this morning, and I'll see that he gets this.'' She offered him a conciliatory smile as he gave her the letter.

''Thank you,'' he said, sounding relieved. He gave her a quick little salute and dashed out to the big white truck with its flashy red, white, and blue logo painted along the side.

Kristi closed the door, glancing at the business-looking letter before she laid it on the narrow table in her entryway. All that was typed on the envelope was Chad's name and address. There was nothing to indicate where it had come from or who had sent it. Nothing about it looked important, or even very interesting. Yet somebody wanted Chad to get it in a hurry. Maybe he was being notified that he'd won a raffle or, better than that, a trip for two to Disneyworld. She giggled out loud thinking Mickey would really love that!

Kristi ambled lazily back, to get dressed. Then she ate a leisurely breakfast and read the newspaper before she felt energized sufficiently to start her Saturday chores. She picked up and did a bit of cleaning around the house, then she drove to the mall to do her weekly grocery shopping. While she was out she also stopped at a jewelry store and had a new battery put in her watch. When the jeweler set the time and handed her watch back to her, she was surprised to discover it was twelve thirty-five.

She drove straight home, parked in the drive, and was just starting to unload her groceries when Chad came out his front door.

"Hi there. Let me give you a hand with that," he said, as his long strides brought him to her side in two seconds flat. "I was wondering where you'd gone. I've been keeping an eye out for you ever since I got back at noon and saw that your car was gone." He reached in the back of the car as he talked, grabbing up three of the five sacks of groceries. "Looks like you've made quite a haul here. Hope you've got something in here I can eat."

"How does new and improved multigrain dog chow grab you?" she teased, giving him an arch look.

"I had something more like a bacon and tomato sandwich in mind. And I'll even furnish the bacon."

"Sounds like a pretty fair deal. Will you cook it too, and not burn it?" she asked playfully.

He grinned. "I'll give it my best shot. Just don't ask me to peel the tomato. Juicy wet things slip out of my hands."

"I'll handle the tomato then, 'cause I've got a fresh-scrubbed kitchen floor. I'll also toast the bread," she declared as she led him into her kitchen. "Now put your sacks of groceries on the counter," she directed. "I'll set mine here on the floor while I get the milk and fresh things in the refrigerator."

"Tell me where you want the dog food and canned stuff and I'll put that away."

"No, that's okay. It's easier if I just do it."

"Hey, are you saying I can't take direction and do a good job?" He made a dejected face. "I really want to be helpful."

She had squatted down and had the refrigerator door open, stowing produce in the vegetable bins. "I'm saying I'd rather do it myself because I'm a kitchen freak. I've got a special spot for each thing." She sidled a look at him, her lips curving in an apologetic smile. "Anyway, there's something important you need to go get. I signed for an overnight mail letter that they brought this morning when you weren't home. It's on the table in my entryway."

"Hmm." Chad looked intrigued. Express mail, huh? Sounds interesting."

"Yeah. You probably won a big prize or something."

"With my luck, it's apt to be a deed to swamp-land in the Florida Everglades," he said.

"Well, go have a look at it and find out. After all, it's important enough that someone wanted you to get it in a hurry." She waved him off. "I'll have this done by the time you've read whatever it is, and then you can tell me all about it if you want to while I peel and you fry."

Chad went to get his mail, then came back to tell Kristi he was going over to his side to check the letter out and get the bacon. Once he'd gone, Kristi made short order of putting the rest of the groceries away. She was just washing her hands in preparation for slicing tomatoes for lunch when Chad came in through the sliding glass door. He had a pound of bacon in his right hand and the express envelope in his left.

"Take a look at this," he said, depositing the letter on the countertop. "I want to see what you'll make of it."

"It isn't bad news, is it?"

"No, I wouldn't say so. It's interesting, but there are some aspects that seem odd." A serious expression tightened his lips.

Chad's words fired her curiosity. She dried her

hands off and immediately removed some official-looking papers from the envelope, scanning the top one with an inquisitive eye.

"Well my word!" she exclaimed in a surprised voice. "This is Mickey's school record." She shifted the papers. "And this one seems to be his medical history, and the vaccinations and shots he's been given and when he had them. Complete and right up-to-date. Why, this is really good to have. I imagine you'll need all this in order to enroll Mickey in school. Won't you? Isn't that the law or something?"

Chad nodded. "Yeah, they'll require his records all right."

"So." She eyed him questioningly. "What's the problem? I don't get it."

"They're not Mickey's real records. At least not his original ones."

"What makes you think that? His name's on them."

Chad gave her an oblique look. "Better check that name again—closely this time."

She looked back at the first sheet, then at the second. She chewed the corner of her lip as she examined them. "You're right, Chad," she said sheepishly. "They have his name as Michael A. Coleman."

"Right. Which Indicates to me that Mickey is not ever to be connected to the Wyatt name. That's what Jack wanted and it looks like somehow he's been able to manipulate these things around to serve his purpose.''

''You think Mickey's father got these records altered in this way and sent them to you. Is that right?'' Her tone was skeptical.

''Who else could it be, Kristi? Jack's the one who wants me to take care of Mickey. He's the one who said Mickey must now use the Coleman name, and he also realized that I'd need school and health records for Mickey.'' There was a note of impatience in his voice. ''He did it. That's obvious.''

''Of course. I understand that much. What I meant is that since Jack's in hiding, and may even be out of this country by now, how did he arrange to get these records altered? And once he obtained them, how did he manage to have them delivered to you in a way that couldn't be traced back to him?'' She pointed to the express envelope. ''See, there are no markings on this. Nothing to indicate who, where, what, or why.'' She tossed her hands up in a frustrated gesture. ''The whole thing beats me.''

Grim lines gathered around Chad's eyes. ''You really think Jack has left the States?''

''Yeah, don't you?''

He rubbed his thumb and forefinger back and forth across his chin. ''I'll tell you what I think as soon as you show me where you stow your frying pan. 'Cause it's high time we got going on those BLTs. I'm hungry,'' he grumbled.

She bent over and took a teflon skillet from the cupboard beneath the range top. She sensed that Chad was more troubled about this than he wanted to let on.

''Me too,'' she said, heading to the refrigerator for lettuce and tomatoes. ''Want yours with or without mayo?''

''With.''

''And on toast—right?''

''Right.'' He was busy laying strips of bacon in the pan, but when he had adjusted the burner to start it cooking, he said, ''I bet you have the same idea about Jack's whereabouts that I do.''

''Well—I'm going on that cryptic verse about *far away places* that came with Mickey's birthday shirt with the kangaroo on the pocket. I thought that was a pretty fair indication that Jack could be hiding out in Australia somewhere.''

''Yeah.'' He heaved a sigh. ''I think that may well be the case, and I'm afraid of what it's going to mean for Mickey.'' Chad's voice filled with anguish.

''What do you mean?'' she asked, looking up from the tomato she was slicing. ''Mickey is content to be here with you, and when things are safe, he can be with his father again.''

Chad shook his head. "I wouldn't count on that."

His words and his grave expression bothered her. "You don't believe something dire is going to happen to Jack, do you?"

"I hope not. What I think is that Jack is taking drastic measures to insure a good and safe life for Mickey as well as for himself."

"And to do this you believe he'll stay permanently in Australia, or someplace other than the U.S., right?" Her voice rose inquiringly.

Chad nodded. "I'd bet that's more or less his plan."

"So what's wrong with that? I'm sure he'll arrange for Mickey to come live with him wherever he is."

"That's the point. I'm ninety-nine percent certain that Jack has no intention of doing that. He's going to take himself out of Mickey's life," he said in a harsh, raw voice.

Kristi's mouth opened in dismay. "Oh no! Surely you're wrong."

"I'm afraid I'm exactly right. When I looked at those records he sent me and saw what Mickey's name is now, I knew what Jack was telling me."

She stared at him, totally bewildered. "His name—how does that tell you anything?"

"I'll explain it to you," he said, turning the bacon and lowering the heat under the frying pan.

"You recall on the medical record it had Michael A. Coleman, and on the school record where they have first name, middle, and last, it was Michael Allen. Well, Allen was our Dad's name, and both Catherine and I have Allen for our middle name." He paused, studying her face in his direct, serious way. "So, making Mickey's middle name Allen like mine and Catherine's was Jack's way of telling me that he's giving his son into my care from now on. Under his present circumstances, he knew that this is what Catherine would want him to do." He let out a long, audible breath, then added in a quieter voice. "It's strange—even prophetic somehow. Because that last summer when my sister and Mickey were here visiting me, Catherine made me promise that if anything happened to her and Jack that I'd take Mickey and raise him as my own."

"And you can do that," she said, smiling softly at him. "You'll give Mickey a good, solid, happy family life."

"Good and solid maybe—but I'll need your help to come up with that normal happy family part." Chad's eyes met hers as he stated this, and there was a tenderness in his gaze that caused her heart to start to hammer. . . .

Chapter Eleven

"I want you to come with me to pick up Mickey at Greta's late this afternoon," Chad said after they'd finished lunch. 'Course, Mickey will bend your ears every minute on the drive back recounting all the fun he's had. Do you think you can take a recital of the Fun Park events? Mickey's going to be excited and nonstop talkative." He casually entwined his fingers behind his head and lounged back in his chair, chuckling as he said this.

"Sounds like fun to me, and I'd like to come with you if I can. I do have an appointment to get my hair cut this afternoon, though. What time would you be going?"

"Oh, about four o'clock, or four-fifteen. I'm

supposed to pick him up no later than five. Can
you make four-fifteen?''

''I don't know. I'll try to get back by then, but
if I'm not here by exactly that time, you leave
without me. Okay?''

''Okay,'' he agreed.

Kristi liked the idea of driving to Kennett Square
with Chad, but she was afraid the timing was going
to be close. She'd had a hair stylist in Baltimore
who gave her the perfect cut for her hair, and she'd
been trying to find someone here that she'd like as
well. She'd waited two weeks to get this appointment today at a beauty shop that had been highly
recommended to her. The shop was not in Marlborough, but in another suburb of Philadelphia
which was at least a twenty-minute drive away.

Ready to leave, Kristi was backing out of the
driveway when she saw Sybil's sleek, silver-gray
Lexus heading for the duplex. It was not a welcome sight. In fact, she suddenly felt as let down
as a bursted balloon. She knew as well as anything
that Sybil would maneuver it so that she was the
one to drive with Chad to Kennett Square. With a
dejected sigh, she drove off, realizing that there
was really not much of a chance that she would
be able to get her hair done and be back in time
to go with him anyway. And Sybil would be there,

so Chad would have no excuse. He'd have to ask
her to go with him to pick up Mickey.

As it turned out, there was even more traffic than
she'd expected for a Saturday afternoon, and it was
four thirty-five when she returned to Marlborough.
Sybil's car was still there, parked in front of the
duplex, and Chad's side of the garage was empty.
Her only consolation was that she'd gotten a fabulous haircut and a blow-dry styling that looked
great on her.

Alex was waiting at the back porch door, anxious to be let in. Kristi welcomed his company; he
was a pleasant distraction from her disappointed
feelings at not going with Chad. Of course, had
she gotten back in time, that would have placed
Chad in the embarrassing position of having to
take both her and Sybil with him. The picture of
Chad, Sybil, and herself driving together made her
chuckle. With Sybil along, the trip would have
been about as much fun as listening to a hinge
squeak. And for poor Mickey on the trip back
home, it would prove about as comfortable as
standing out in the pouring rain.

Kristi had a deadline on a series of Alexander
the Small comic strips. She carried a can of cola
into the back room and settled down to work for
a couple of hours. Alex came with her and
stretched out on the rug underneath her drawing

board. Kristi had adopted Alex from an animal shelter when he was just a three-or four-month-old puppy. In those early months, he chewed up everything he could get a hold of, which included Kristi's drawing tablets and her pens and pencils. It took only one such episode and then her work area was definitely off limits for Alexander. It wasn't until almost a year later, after he'd matured, gone through obedience training, and become a well-behaved companion as well as Kristi's model for Alexander the Small, that he earned the privilege of having his own special place close to Kristi when she was creating her cartoons.

For the next two hours, Kristi concentrated all her thoughts on her creative tasks. Fortunately, the ideas she had in her mind came together well, and the resulting sketches pleased her. She worked until seven, then microwaved a teriyaki chicken dinner and carried it into the living room to eat in front of the television.

A short time later, she thought she heard a car door slam, and a moment later, there was someone knocking at her front door. The instant she opened the door, Mickey burst out talking.

"I'm supposed to ask you if I can stay here for a while," he piped in a high, agitated voice. "They're having a big fight out there that they don't want me to listen to. Sybil called it a discussion, but it's a fight. And Uncle Chad's real mad about the things she's said. He doesn't want me to hear any more of what Sybil says—that's for sure.'' He poured all of this out in a rapid clip of words.

Over Mickey's head Kristi could see Chad and Sybil standing by the side of his car, and from the decisive movements of Sybil's head and Chad's rigid, defensive stance, it certainly did appear that there was an argument going on.

She quickly grabbed Mickey's arm, urging him inside, and immediately closed the door. The last thing she wanted was to appear to be watching whatever was going on in the driveway.

''I guess it's my fault,'' Mickey continued nervously. ''I shouldn't have told Sybil that I was going to stay here and go to school. Wow, that was sure the last thing she wanted to hear.'' He wagged his head, a hurt expression in his eyes. ''She sure doesn't want me around where she is. I suppose that's 'cause she doesn't like me very much.''

Kristi hugged his trembling shoulders. ''Hey now, she likes you. I think it's just that she's not used to being around kids—doesn't know how to talk to a boy your age. And besides, I'm sure none of it is your fault. Don't even think that it is,'' she said, taking his hand and leading him over to sit down on the couch with her. ''You know, Mickey, I think that Sybil was just completely surprised to hear the good news that you'd be living here with Chad and going to school here this fall.''

''She was surprised, all right. Boy, she sounded off about it too. Made a bunch of cracks until Chad told her to knock it off.'' Mickey looked up at her, a puzzled expression on his freckled face. ''Say, what is a built-in nanny anyhow?''

Kristi gasped in surprise. ''A what?''

''A built-in nanny. Sybil told Chad that she supposed the next thing he was going to do was take me on permanently since he already had such a convenient built-in nanny. So what is that exactly?''

Kristi's face colored fiercely, for she was momentarily abashed at the implication of Sybil's spiteful words. ''Well, a—a nanny is a person who looks after children—like a nurse—or a governess,'' she stammered as she struggled to conceal the emotions that this had stirred up in her, and answer Mickey's question in a composed and normal voice. ''She's someone who sees after a child's needs, like seeing that he has clean clothes to wear, good food to eat, gives him care and attention, things like that.''

Mickey's eyes sparkled in comprehension. ''You mean like Greta does for me.''

''Yes—a little like that. But, of course, Greta does more. She keeps house and takes care of things for Chad, too.''

"Guess that's why she's a built-in nanny, because she looks after both of us." He grinned, acting pleased as punch to have figured it all out for himself.

"Well, I don't really know, and it's not all that important anyway," Kristi said, passing it off with a shrug. "Now, I want to hear about all the things you and Greta's grandsons got to do at the Fun Park. Tell me first about the boys. What are their names?" she asked quickly, wanting to get Mickey's mind off of Sybil and the nanny bit.

"Karl is the one that's older. He's ten, and he's really cool. He's probably going to play little league baseball at school this year. And Otto's only seven, but he's a neat little kid. He's got red hair, so everybody calls him Red Ott. Whenever they call him, it sounds like they're saying *Red Hot*, and it's really funny." Mickey let out a ripple of happy laughter recalling this. Now that he was off on a happy subject, his earlier tense expression vanished. He talked excitedly about everything that he, Karl, and Red Ott had done, describing each of the rides at the Fun Park in great detail.

A short time later, Chad came to get him. "I'm sorry I dumped Mickey on you this way," he said as he came in. "But it was really necessary to get him out of earshot. He'd heard enough to harm him already." There were tight lines that ran from his nostrils to the corners of his mouth, evidence of the tension Chad was under.

"That was perfectly all right. I'm glad I was here and could help you out," she said, leading him from the entry hall into the living room. In fact, I've been enjoying hearing a rundown on Mickey's sleepover at Greta's and the big time he had with the boys in Lancaster. Sounds like a great time was had by all." She turned to Mickey and smiled. "That's right, isn't it, Mick?"

He grinned and got up from the couch and walked over to where Chad stood. "It was super-cool all right!"

"Sounded that way, although I haven't had a chance to get a full report as yet, have I, Mick?" Chad said, putting his arm around the boy's shoulders. "So let's go home and talk, and let Kristi get back to what she was doing."

Kristi made no attempt to detain them. In fact, she was anxious to have them gone so she could think about what had happened here and consider the implications of what Mickey had repeated to her. Bless his heart, in his childish innocence, of course, he couldn't know how much Sybil's words could hurt her.

"I'll see you and explain about all this later," Chad said, as he and Mickey walked to the door.

Kristi shook her head. Hearing about it from Chad was the last thing she wanted. "That's not necessary, Chad. I think I understand fairly well from the few things Mickey said. Obviously learning that Mickey was going to live with you this year and go to school here came as a big surprise to Sybil. I think she was caught off guard and said things she probably didn't mean.''

Chad scrutinized Kristi, an intent, questioning look in his eyes. ''You give her more credit than I do,'' he said bluntly. ''That's all I can say.''

He and Mickey left then, and Kristi locked the front door after them. She walked slowly back to the living room and sank down onto the sofa. For a few minutes, she closed her eyes, rubbing them lightly with her fingertips. When she opened them, her expression was bleak. She'd bet that Sybil's mother hadn't wasted one minute before reporting that she and Ed had run into Chad and her last night at Nicolette's. That in itself accounted for why Sybil showed up at Chad's this afternoon. Apparently Sybil felt she took first priority on Chad's time and attentions. It would incense Sybil that Chad had taken her out to dinner, especially to someplace as elegant and expensive as Nicolette's. Picturing Sybil's jealous reaction when she learned this made Kristi smile and feel just a trifle smug, at least for an instant.

Her complacency vanished as she thought about Sybil referring to her as a built-in nanny. No doubt Sybil, in angry frustration, felt this was a clever phrase to toss out to further irritate Chad. Still, it made Kristi stop and think. She knew she'd admitted to herself early on that Chad desired her company in a large part because of Mickey. She didn't doubt that Chad found her attractive and fun. And he felt something for her, he was making that more apparent all the time. But at the most, their relationship was a comfortable, caring friendship that brought security and happiness into the life of a nine-year-old boy. She might hope for more, but she didn't dare count on it. She was already more vulnerable where Chad was concerned than she ought to be.

Determined to put tonight's episode out of her mind, Kristi reached for the television remote and began searching the channels for a movie, hopefully one she hadn't seen half a dozen times before. She was about to settle for Doris Day in *With Six You Get Eggroll* when her telephone rang. When she answered it, she was suprised and quite pleased to find it was Derek Dryden. The last couple of times Derek had asked her out, she'd been unable to go. Since that was more than three weeks ago, she had begun to think he'd given up on her.

"Derek, I'm so glad to hear from you," she told him, letting her pleasure show in the warm tone of her voice. "How are things going?"

"Pretty good. I just got back from two weeks' vacation."

"Lucky you. Where did you go?"

"To a fishing camp way up in northern Ontario. My dad and my brother and I go there for ten days every summer. It's become a tradition with the male members of my family. And while we men are up in the Canadian wilds roughing it, my mother and my two sisters go to New York and see a bunch of Broadway shows and shop," he said, a smile in his voice. "That's what keeps us a big happy family."

She laughed. "Sounds like you've found the right formula to please both genders."

"It works fine for ten days, but now I've had enough of the old male bonding and I want to spend time with a pretty girl for a change. I'm hoping you'll go eat pizza with me tomorrow and take in a movie. How does that sound to you?"

"Sounds good, Derek, but I'd like to alter the plan a little. Let me fix dinner for us here at my place. I'd really like to do that, and I do have a good VCR, so you rent a movie for us to see. Would you go for that?" Her invitation was so spontaneous it simply rolled off her tongue, almost without her volition.

"Why—sure, that would be great. I—I mean, I'd really like to do that." He sounded surprised that she'd offered to cook dinner for him. And as a matter of fact, she was a little surprised that she'd done it too. . . .

Chapter Twelve

Late the following afternoon, Kristi got busy in the kitchen, preparing a shrimp and wild rice casserole to have ready to slip in the oven when Derek came. Also, she spread thick slices of French bread with herb and garlic butter, then put a wooden bowl of mixed salad greens in the refrigerator to be tossed with dressing and topped with seasoned croutons. This menu, with the coffee ice cream she'd bought for dessert, she felt would make a nice Sunday night supper for her and Derek.

She hadn't actually figured out just why she'd issued her invitation to him last night, but now the more she thought about it the more certain she was that it had been a good move on her part. In the first place, Derek had taken her out now a number of times, and it was her turn to reciprocate. Besides that, she certainly needed to cultivate new friends. Now that she was going to be living and working in Philadelphia, she owed it to herself to meet people and socialize with them at every opportunity. Much as she enjoyed and wanted to be involved in Chad and Mickey's lives, she'd be a fool to exclude some other attractive man without taking an opportunity to become acquainted with him.

Now she set the table in the dining room with blue place mats and silverware. She was just reaching up to a high shelf in a kitchen cabinet to get two blue water goblets when Chad tapped on the glass door before sliding it open and entering her kitchen.

"Hi," he said, coming over to stand behind her and placing his hands on her shoulders. "You look busy for a lazy Sunday," he said, gently caressing her shoulders.

"I have been busy, but as soon as I put these on the table," she held up the pair of goblets, "I'll be through." She walked past him into the dining room and set a glass at each place, then turned and came back.

"I was going to grill hamburgers later on, and I hoped you'd join me and Mickey for dinner. However, it looks like you've got other plans." A suggestion of a frown flitted across his brow.

Kristi nodded. "Yes, I have a friend coming over for dinner."

"Look, if you're planning to use the charcoaler on the porch, that's fine!" he said emphatically. "I mean it. It's high time you had your turn, and the undisturbed use of the porch. I'll take Mickey for a Big Mac, which he'll like better anyway."

"Oh no," she said, shaking her head. "We won't be outside. I've got the food all ready to go into the oven."

He looked concerned. "Are you sure? Because you know you can have the use of the charcoaler anytime, and we share the porch fifty-fifty. So don't you dare hesitate to tell me when you want to use it, and I'll stay clear. That's a promise."

Chad had spoken all this so earnestly that she couldn't keep from smiling at him. "I know that, Chad. You're certainly very nice and very thoughtful, but my cooking expertise is limited to a few choice recipes out of the Make It Now, Bake It Later Cookbook," she said jokingly. "So you can go right ahead tonight and grill your hamburgers outside, and I won't get in your way."

He laughed. "And I'll keep Mickey from horning in on you and your friend. Of course, Mickey is going to be curious as a cat to find out if your friend is a gal or a guy," he said, slanting his head and eyeing her slyly.

"Oh now really, Chad, a nine-year-old boy

wouldn't care about that any more than you would," she said facetiously. "And I'm sure that you're not interested in knowing that my dinner guest is a nice fellow who happens to be the brother of one of the artists I work with at Word Wise."

Chad grinned sheepishly. "I guess I didn't fool you for a minute, did I?"

She shrugged and pressed her lips together in a Mona Lisa smile.

"Well, you can't blame me for wanting to size up the competition."

This had become a rather silly conversation, so Kristi ignored Chad's last statement and abruptly turned her back, opened the freezer top of the refrigerator, and removed two trays of ice. "I think I'll put these in my ice bucket and freeze the trays again. Can't have too much ice on hand in this kind of weather," she commented inanely.

Chad took the hint. "You've got things to do, I know. Just let me say one thing about Mickey, and then I'll get out of your way."

"That's okay. I've got forty-five minutes before Derek will get here," she countered quickly. "And I do want to know how things went with Mickey after you two left here. He tried not to show it, but I think he was pretty upset."

"Yeah, I know he was. He had every right to be too, after the less than subtle remarks Sybil made in the car driving home from Greta's.'' There was a bitter edge to his troubled voice. ''I was worried about how he'd take it, but Mickey's one game little guy. Maybe it's because of all he's been through with Jack since Catherine died, but he's learned how to roll with the punches.'' He paused, taking a second to search her face. His gaze was contemplative. ''Also, I think it made Mickey feel much better when I assured him that there'd be no cause for him to be around Sybil anymore.''

It was her turn to silently question him with her eyes. Just how was he going to handle that, she wondered. She hesitated for a minute, then said, ''It's probably a good idea that you see Sybil alone and do things with her away from your house, at least for a time. That will be easier on Mickey.''

Chad shook his head. ''You don't understand. I'm not going be doing anything at all with Sybil.''

''But I thought—I mean you and Sybil are—''

He interrupted her. ''Let me tell you what we are. We're friends on a sort of standby basis. You see, Sybil and I have a group of the same friends, and we share some of the same interests. So for those reasons I've been a convenient date for her for social events, and for art shows at her gallery where she likes to have a man at her side. This worked out fine until now, because neither one of us was involved with anyone special. But this summer things are entirely different. My life has changed in every way. I'm sure you know that by now, Kristi.'' His voice was suddenly smoky soft, and his glance appealing. ''You'll never hear me complain about rainy days. They are the luckiest of all for me.'' He smiled, and then his warm chuckle reverberated through her, causing an unexpected ripple of contentment to touch her heart. In the moment that followed, Chad took her face in his hands, and the next instant his lips settled against hers. Though the kiss was brief, Kristi experienced an intimacy in it that made any rational thought she might have dissolve into dreamy bits.

After Chad left, Kristi would have liked to sit down quietly and think about everything he had said, but, of course, she couldn't let herself do that. Derek would be coming anytime now, and she wasn't quite ready for him. She wanted to change her clothes, wear something suitable for the hostess of an at-home dinner for two. So she put her thoughts about Chad on hold, and hurried off to her bedroom to don a pair of cream-colored slacks, a matching short-sleeved silk shirt, and a Hawaiian print vest in island colors of cerise, aqua, lavender, and canary yellow.

Derek arrived promptly at six-thirty, bearing not only the promised movie video, but also a gift for Alex. It was an intriguing thing with surefire appeal for any dog. It was made of strips of genuine rawhide braided together and formed into a bow-knot. "Alex will love that," Kristi told him. "You're mighty nice to bring my pet a special treat."

"That's part of my strategy. Make friends with your dog so he won't run me off," he said, smiling like a politician.

. Kristi laughed. "Sounds like you speak from experience."

"Let's say past encounters have made me cautious."

"Well, you have nothing to worry about from Alex. He's friendly and quite affectionate when you get to know him."

"And how about you? Are you the same?"

"Let's say past experience makes me somewhat more reserved than my anxious-to-please terrier," she countered facetiously. They both laughed. "Now Derek, I'll call Alex and you can go outside on the porch and give him his present and get acquainted with him while I do some last-minute things about our dinner." She led him to the sliding glass doors as she spoke and ushered him outside.

Derek remained outdoors for perhaps ten minutes. When he came back inside the amused smile that curved his lips echoed the glint of humor in his blue eyes. "I've just been checked out and thoroughly interrogated by a very inquisitive young man who I must say has a most proprietary attitude toward both you and your dog. More than that, I think I'd be right to say that he has what amounts to a mammoth crush on you, Kristi.''

She smiled. ''If he's about nine years old with blond hair and a saddle of freckles spanning his nose and cheeks, he's my *rainy day* friend from next door, and I'm a bit smitten with him too,'' she said, laughing.

''Well, he didn't seem to keen on my being here. He said he always looked after Alex, but that he'd been told not to bother you and your company tonight.''

Kristi smiled inwardly at this. Evidently Chad had kept his word about telling Mickey he mustn't horn in on her tonight, or peer through the glass to look at her dinner guest. But since Derek had gone outside on the porch, that made him fair game for Mickey. He'd gotten the chance to give Derek the once-over and still he hadn't actually disobeyed Chad's orders. She couldn't help but chuckle at the thought of Mickey giving Derek the third degree. Furthermore, she would be curious to know just how much Mickey would report to Chad. . . .

Chapter Thirteen

In the remaining days of August, summer laziness was giving way to a new time. The grass was yellowing and there was a start of new color in the deep woods around Marlborough. Small whiffs of cool air, a downy woodpecker squawking, the changing color in a sumac or two, all these things were little hints that autumn was only weeks away.

Derek had to do a great deal of traveling in his job, and consequently Kristi had only been out with him twice since the Sunday he'd been to dinner at her place. This was probably just as well, because she sensed that he was beginning to get serious about her, and she shouldn't let that happen. Not as long as she felt the way she did about Chad. Maybe she had made a big mistake to let herself become so involved in Chad and Mickey's lives. Maybe she could get hurt, badly hurt, but it was a chance she'd have to take. Besides, it was too late. She cared so much for Mickey, and she was totally in love with Chad.

In these past weeks, Chad made a date with Kristi for every Thursday night, when Greta was there to stay with Mickey. And on Saturdays, if Kristi was free, she took part in whatever Mickey and Chad had planned for their weekend activity, always ending with a hamburger cookout in the backyard. These were halcyon days for Kristi.

The Saturday after Chad got Mickey all enrolled in school, he enlisted Kristi to go with the two of them on a school shopping spree. First on Mickey's need list was a navy blue backpack to fill with all of his required school supplies. After this was accomplished, Chad suggested that while the two of them shopped for back to school clothes, he would do the week's grocery shopping.

"Kristi, Mick knows the kind of stuff he wants, and I figure something like three or four pairs of pants, with say six shirts to match up with them, and another pair of those special brand shoes he idolizes," Chad said, smiling and handing a fistful of bills to Kristi. "A few pair of socks and that ought to do it," he added quickly. "But I'm flexible on this. So get him what you think he should have, but don't get too carried away, 'cause you have to quit when this money runs out. You understand?''

Mickey bobbed his head. ''We understand, don't we Kristi?''

She nodded afirmatively. ''We'll shop wisely and keep to our allowance,'' she said gaily, and taking Mickey's hand, the two of them left Chad and marched off in the direction of the major department store located at the far end of the mall.

An hour and forty-five minutes later, Chad was waiting in the designated spot to pick them up. He quickly opened up the trunk of the car as Kristie and Mickey, loaded down with shopping bags, approached.

''Wait till you see all the great stuff that we got,'' Mickey said, grinning from ear to ear. ''You won't believe it.''

''I'm afraid I'll have to.'' Chad grimaced in good humor as he stowed all the parcels in the trunk.

''We got things that we didn't even have on the list! Didn't we, Kristi?''

She nodded, and turned to Chad. ''We found a couple of items that we decided were really needed, so I thought we could make a slight substitution or two.''

''Yeah, I got a really cool new jacket and the neatest sweater you ever saw,'' Mickey said, wiggling with excitement like a dog with two tails.

"And I see you also bought a baseball cap," Chad said, eyeing the bright blue cap Mickey was sporting, turned around with the visor in the back.

"That was a freebie, Chad," Kristi hastened to inform him. They gave it to him when he bought his super sport shoes. And get this, the shoes were even on sale, at twenty-five percent off. How's that for a bargain!"

"Not bad at all. And may I add that I feel better knowing that my hard-earned money has been well spent and not a penny was wasted on the fad of the moment—the baseball cap." There was teasing laughter in his eyes, and his mouth twitched in amusement.

"I think your uncle is having a little fun with us, Mickey, don't you?"

"He just likes to tease me about the things kids wear now. He doesn't understand what's really cool, but that's okay," Mickey said, as the three of them climbed in the car. "Maybe it's time to tell him about our surprise."

"Yeah, I expect it is. The laugh will be on him then, Mickey," she said, giving the boy a conspiratory wink. "So you go ahead and tell him."

"What are you two going on about, anyway?" Chad asked, arching an eyebrow at them as he started the car.

"There's something we discovered when we got all through shopping that we haven't told you about yet. You're probably going to be plenty surprised too," Mickey said, obviously making it sound as important as he could.

"Well, you've got me guessing. You told me you got all the clothes you had on your list, plus a jacket, a sweater, and even a baseball cap. I have no idea what else there could possibly be." Chad shrugged, looking totally mystified.

Appearing delighted with Chad's reaction, Mickey said rather dramatically, "The surprise is that we bought it all and even had money left over——eighteen dollars and sixty-seven cents——I know 'cause I counted it myself."

"That's remarkable! I have to say, you and Kristi are the most budget-conscious, super shoppers to be found anywhere. And the beautiful part about this is discovering that I can afford you both and not go broke." Chad laughed in a deep, jovial way. His laugh was marvelously catching, and the three of them filled the car with the happy sound of their shared laughter.

By the time school started for Mickey, there was a sudden cooling in the nights and something different in the slant of morning light. This turn of season put the squirrels to work burying nuts with a new urgency. In the backyard of the duplex, the garden was dry and browning, the flowers finished, the leaves of an apple tree had started spinning down, and the light fall breeze sent acorns rattling across a carpet of dry oak leaves. Indeed, it was time again to savor autumn.

That Thursday afternoon, as Kristi drove from her office to the courthouse, she was filled with curiosity. Why, she wondered, was Chad so insistent that she be with him when he talked with this federal marshal, who had come from Washington that morning? She'd asked him why on the phone, but all he said was that he'd explain when he saw her, and that it was important to him that she be there.

Chad was standing on the steps of the courthouse waiting for her when she arrived. He grabbed her hands, drawing her to one side. ''Let me brief you on this before we go inside,'' he said quickly. ''This man's name is Travis Hensley. All he told me when he called to set up this appointment was that we needed to talk about my nephew and the plans that the boy's father wishes me to carry out. That's the way he put it. He never called either Jack or Mickey by name.''

''That seems strange, doesn't it?'' Kristi frowned, looking puzzled.

''Yeah, that's what I thought, so I got a lawyer friend of mine whose father is a judge to check this Hensley fellow's credentials. Guess what? He's a federal marshal with the Witness Protection Program. Strictly legit.''

"Do you think this means that they've arranged protection for Jack?" she asked thoughtfully.

"I think it's a strong possibility. And it certainly would explain how I got those official new school and health records for Michael Allen Coleman." He glanced at his watch and urged her up the steps. "Come on, it's time to go. We're supposed to meet him in room 209 in three minutes."

They took the elevator to the second floor and discovered the room they were looking for was just two doors down the hall to the right. Kristi and Chad entered a well-furnished room that bore the appearance of a lawyer's office and library, for its mahogany-paneled walls were lined with shelves of impressive leather-bound books. Sitting there with his elbows on the desk and his chin resting on his fist was the man they'd come to meet. He presented a clear and unblurred profile, almost as though he were posing for their inspection. His head was well-shaped, and his hair had that thick silver-fox look of a person who had started to gray early in life. His deep-set eyes were darkly shadowed, his nose long and aquiline, his mouth pleasant, the chin strongly formed, and, from the length of his wrist emerging from a white shirt cuff, and the way he disposed of his legs beneath the narrow desk, Kristi guessed that he was tall, probably over six feet. He took his hand from his chin, pushed back his shirt cuff to consult his watch, and smiled.

"You two are right on time, and I thank you for that. I've been offered a helicopter ride back to Washington later this afternoon, and since you're so prompt, I'll have no trouble making it." His smile deepened, etching lines down his cheeks and creasing up his eyes. He got to his feet as he spoke and now extended his hand to Chad. "Nice to meet you, Coleman, and this must be the young woman you told me about who's so fond of Michael," he said, turning his attention now to Kristi. "So, won't you both sit down, and we'll get right to the purpose of our meeting."

It was impossible not to be warmed by the older man's charm. Kristie glanced at Chad and was relieved to see that he looked at ease, and as if he sensed there would be a nice rapport between the three of them.

"Now, of course, it's the young boy's care and welfare that we're all interested in, but before we get into that, I bet you'd like me to tell you what part I play in this whole situation. Right?"

"That would certainly help," Chad said, with a wry chuckle. "We're pretty much in the dark. I'd appreciate knowing as much about my brother-in-law as you feel you can tell me."

Hensley's manner was entirely serious and businesslike now. "I'm sure you've figured out that we have him in Witness Protection, which means that there no longer is a Jack Wyatt. We've erased him, so to speak. He has a new identity now, and a new life.''

"From a birthday card that came in a gift to Mickey, Chad and I figured he was somewhere out of this country. Probably in Australia,'' Kristi interjected. "Can you tell us if that's true?''

He shook his head. "You must understand that I can't reveal his new identity to anyone, nor intimate where he might or might not be at the present time. There will not be any direct contact between him and his son. That's where I come in. My part is to act as liaison. He will communicate with you and with Michael through me. Likewise, any message or information regarding Michael that you want relayed to him will pass through me. Actually, that's the purpose of our meeting together. I have a letter for you from your brother-in-law in which he explains all the reasons why he feels it's in Michael's best interests to be with you permanently. And of course this is what he wants for the boy if you are willing and would be able to take him.'' As the marshal said this, he picked up two envelopes off the desk and handed them to Chad. "He's also sent a letter here for Michael which he wants you to read and determine if it should be given to the boy now or kept until a later time. It's to be your decision.''

Chad took the letters, a musing expression on his face. "I've been in a quandary as to exactly

what I should tell Mickey about his dad's problems. I trust Jack explains what he wants Mickey
to know in this letter.''

"Yes, he does, but he's assuming that you
are going to agree to become Michael's legal
guardian.''

"Of course I am. I've even anticipated this.
Once I learned about what led up to Jack's going
into hiding, I realized both his and Mickey's safety
depended on his leaving Mickey with me and hiding out alone.''

"You're absolutely right about that,'' Hensley
agreed. "And, of course, that is the reason for
changing Michael's name and altering all records
so there will be nothing to connect him to a person
named Jack Wyatt. Everything possible has been
done to shield the boy, I assure you.''

"I'm sure of that, and I'm grateful. I love
Mickey, and I intend to provide a normal and sta-
ble environment for him. You tell Jack that I will
take the best possible care of Mickey, and I'll
make sure he has everything he needs to have a
happy, healthy life.'' Chad's voice had depth and
authority, and no one could doubt his determination to do everything he said he would.

"That's good!'' Hensley exclaimed, a well-
satisfied ring in his voice. "I couldn't agree more
that this is the ideal solution for all concerned. I

will immediately take care of the legal details to make you Mickey's guardian.''

''You know how I look at this, Chad,'' Kristi said, smiling at him, her eyes a bit misty and wistful. ''You and Jack are sort of switching places in Mickey's life. You're taking the part of the parent, and Jack becomes the devoted relative who will send him letters and presents and whom he may see for visits in the summertime.'' She now turned to the marshal, adding, ''Isn't that rather the way you see it too?''

''Well, somewhat like that,'' he answered evasively, as he rubbed his forefinger back and forth across his chin. ''I imagine there will be occasional letters that I'll forward to the boy, and certainly packages at Christmas and on his birthday.'' He paused—I do recall sending a gift on to him from his father several weeks ago for his birthday.'' He gave Kristi a brief nod and smile. ''But I doubt Michael would be able to visit him. Not in the near future, that's for sure. So don't even suggest to Michael that seeing his father is a possibility, please,'' he said, underlining each word in an emphatic tone of voice.

The three of them talked only a few minutes longer to cover a couple of minor details. Then, since the purpose of their meeting had been accomplished, and the federal marshal had a helicopter ride to catch, Chad, Kristi, and Travis Hensley left the office and took the elevator to the main floor of the courthouse together.

Chapter Fourteen

"You don't have to go back to work, do you?" Chad asked as they walked down the court-house steps to reach the sidewalk.

"I suppose I should. What time is it anyway?" She paused and held her arm up to see her watch. "Oh my, it's a quarter of four," she muttered, answering her own question. "By the time I get my car and drive back to Word Wise, it's going to be a quarter after, at least."

"Exactly," Chad concurred. "And by the time you get your materials back on your drawing board, it'll be four-thirty, and quitting time is five. So, my opinion is that you couldn't have time to get any more work done today, therefore, what you need to do is come have a cup of coffee with me and we'll talk over all that's just happened." He put his hand on her arm to detain her. "I'll let you read the letters from Jack that Hensley gave me, if you'll come," he tempted her, with a knowing grin. "Bet Mickey's letter would interest you even more than mine. What do you think?"

"I think you're leading me astray," she quipped, with a significant lifting of her brows.

"I'm certainly trying to," he countered. "Am I succeeding?"

"Far better than you know," she answered candidly.

A faintly eager look flashed in his eyes. "That's the most encouraging thing I think you've ever said to me. And it's what I needed most to hear at this very time." There was a gleam of unreadable emotion in his eyes as he spoke.

"What do you mean?" She studied his expression, totally mystified. "I must have missed something. Are we talking on the same wavelength here?"

"I sure hope so. It's something I intend to tell you about later on, angel. But for right now, come with me. I'll get my car and then drive you to your car. You can then follow me to a coffeehouse that's about two or three miles from here. Maybe you've heard of it. It's called The Java Bean."

"No, I haven't. This will be my first trip to a coffeehouse in Philly." She looped her arm through his. "The Java Bean—it does sound rather exotic," she said as they headed across to the underground parking garage a block away.

"It's a bit unusual, all right. Has lots of those beaded curtains and old brass jugs and pots and foreign-looking stuff. It's *trendy* and popular."

"Okay, I'm for it. Let's get going."

Twenty-five minutes later they were seated on bamboo camp stools at a small round wicker table in the somewhat crowded and noisy Java Bean café. Chad had described the atmosphere of the place fairly well. To Kristi it looked like a cross between a South Seas island hut and an Arabian marketplace.

Almost immediately they were served tall slender mugs of rich, aromatic coffee along with a small plate of rice cakes and a cookie that Kristi decided had dates and nuts in the center.

"Now I want to hear what you thought of this Hensley fellow who's going to be a liaison between Jack and us," Chad said, launching their discussion without any further preliminaries.

"I rather liked him. He was friendly, helpful, and most distinguished-looking, with that elegant silver-gray hair. I need to think up a character like him to use in Alexander the Small one day next month."

He made a wry face at her. "Leave it to a female artist to only characterize a man by the color of his hair.''

''I said he was friendly and helpful too,'' she shrugged. ''After all, I only saw the man for an hour. That's hardly time for an in-depth study.'' She wrinkled her nose at him. ''So, since you're so discerning, what did you think of him?'' she teased, smiling coyly.

They exchanged a subtle look of amusement before he answered. ''I liked him. I appreciated it that he gave us as much information about Jack as he did. I really think he told us all he could. Don't you?''

''Yeah, I do. In fact, I think the way he worded his comment when I told him we thought Jack might be in Australia, led me to feel that we were right, but he just couldn't tell us we were.''

''That could be true. I do think that there's no doubt that Jack is no longer in the United States.''

''Well the good part is that with the aid of this man, Mickey will have contact with his father. This is so important for his happiness, Chad. He's already lost his mother, poor little guy.'' A tone of sadness entered her voice now. ''It's absolutely vital that he knows his father is safe out there somewhere, and that although it's a long time off, at least one of these days he will see him again.'' Kristi's voice broke slightly. ''You do believe Mickey will see Jack again, don't you?''

Chad reached out and touched her hand. "I don't know, Kristi," he answered, his voice grave and low. "I hope and pray he will."

She stared at him in dismay. "But you really don't believe he will—do you?"

He shook his head regretfully. "I'm afraid we shouldn't count on it," he said with quiet emphasis. He let go of her hand and pushed Jack's letter toward her. "Read this."

She hesitated, studying Chad's expressive face for a moment before picking up the letter. "Did something in Jack's letter upset you?" she asked.

"No. It surprised me, that's all." He picked up his coffee mug, and also reached for one of the rice cakes. "Take your time and read it."

It was not a long letter, about a sheet and a half. The first page reiterated what the federal marshal had already told them concerning Jack's specific plea for Chad to take legal guardianship of Mickey. It was an unhesitatingly frank letter and Kristi could sense the emotional pain Jack had to go through to write it. She turned to the second page and as she read the final poignant lines, the words became blurred across the paper as her eyes welled with sympathetic tears. She saw now what had surprised Chad. It was this last sentence, that came straight from an understanding father's loving heart.

If after a year has passed, Chad, you should

wish to legally adopt Mickey, and he feels he would like that too, I want you to know I would readily agree. In fact, for Mickey's happiness and his future life, I could only welcome it and be forever grateful. It was signed simply with a J.

"Jack's letter is very moving," she said, as she folded it carefully and handed it back to Chad. "It's not fair the things that have happened to him. I feel so sorry for him, for Mickey, and for you too, Chad. This can't be easy for anyone."

"It's brought about some changes. That's for sure."

"And possibly there's going to be more to come. But I've got a feeling you can handle it." She appraised him with a complimenting smile.

"I'm going to need you to help me. What I want more than anything else is to have you with me in this." The look on his face mingled eagerness and tenderness.

She looked at him questioningly. "I'll do everything I can to help you with Mickey, if that's what you mean."

"I mean a great deal more than that, Kristi. I'm just waiting for the right time for us to talk about it." There was now a look of implacable determination marking his face.

"You make it sound important."

"It's vitally important to me, and I want it to be the same for you."

Something in the way Chad was regarding her made her breath catch in her throat. She put her hand to her lips and gave a nervous cough, hesitating for a second or two before saying anything. "I don't think either of us would be comfortable talking here. It's much too crowded and noisy," she said finally. "Besides, I need to get home and feed Alex."

"And I need to go too, because Greta and Mickey are waiting on me for dinner."

Chad paid the check and together they walked outside. When they reached Kristi's car, Chad opened the door on the driver's side for her. "Promise me we can take up where we left off when it's the right time and place," he said, touching her cheek gently with the back of his hand.

"I promise," she said, smiling softly as she got in the car.

As Kristi put the key in the ignition, Chad tucked his head down. "I love you," he murmured huskily. Then he closed the door and moved back so she could drive away.

Had Chad actually said what she thought he had? She was wide awake, so she hadn't dreamed it. She had excellent hearing, and even though Chad's voice had been low and husky, he'd lowered his head so it was close to hers, and he'd spoken those three lovely words right in her ear. "I love you," he'd said, and with the thought of it, she could even imagine that she was hearing him say it again. A happy sensation ricocheted through her and she felt as if her heart were singing.

Chad wasn't the sort of man who made glib, insincere statements. If he said it, he meant it. She didn't doubt that he honestly felt a kind of love for her. But there are various sorts of love. Her mind cautioned her to remember that this had been an emotional afternoon that they had shared. Chad had wanted her with him when he met with Travis Hensley because he saw her as the one person who understood the love and responsibility he felt for Mickey. This, coupled with the fact that Chad knew she genuinely cared for Mickey, was undoubtedly the basis of his saying what he'd said. She must be careful not to romanticize it into something more.

Chapter Fifteen

The first day of the following week, Chad was flying to Chicago on business. Greta was to stay at the duplex to take care of Mickey. Kristi volunteered to take Chad to the Philadelphia airport early Monday morning so he could leave his car for Greta to drive Mickey to and from school, and to use for whatever came up that the two of them might want to do while he was gone.

"I'll pick you up when you come home," she said when they reached the terminal. "What time is your return flight?"

"Five something Thursday afternoon. I'll call you about it Wednesday night." He hopped out of her car, and waved her off so she wouldn't be late getting to work.

When she got home from work Monday evening, Eric Mueller's truck was in the driveway. She had barely gotten in the house before Mickey appeared on her side of the porch, knocking on the glass door and calling to her.

"Something bad happened to Red Ott," he exclaimed excitedly. "He's in the hospital getting an operation. Eric says his *pendix* or something like that got busted." He grabbed Kristi's hand, talking all the time as they crossed the porch to Chad's side. "Eric says he's going to Lancaster right now and he says Greta should go with him. Says Red Ott is terrible sick and could die. Greta started crying when he said this. She says she can't leave, 'cause she's taking care of me. But I could stay with you, then she could go be with Red Ott. That would be all right, wouldn't it?" he pleaded, running out of breath after this outpouring of words.

Kristi squeezed his hand reassuringly. "Of course it would, and that's exactly what we're all going to do," she told him emphatically.

Several hours later that night, Kristi's phone rang, and it was Chad calling from Chicago. "Hi," he said, a merry note in his voice. "How's everything going there?"

"Fine," she said in a noncommittal tone.

"I couldn't raise anyone at my place, and I thought I'd like the first-day report. Is everything shipshape around my homestead?'' he asked, with a questioning inflection.

Kristi paused momentarily, debating with herself only for a split second before deciding that there was no reason to tell Chad that Greta was gone. It might upset him, or even make him come home, thus jeopardizing the important business he had in Chicago. To avoid this, she quickly said, ''Oh, Eric came by and he and Greta went off on an errand. Mickey elected to stay and take me on in a game of checkers, which he won. Right now he's outside with Alex. Want me to call him in to talk to you?'' She held her breath hoping he'd say no.

''No, don't do that. ''I really want to talk to you—because, you know something, I find I miss you.''

''That's nice to hear. I'll tell Mickey you miss us.'' There was a smile in her voice.

Chad laughed. ''I miss him too, of course.''

''How are your business deals coming along?'' she quickly asked, wanting to steer their conversation in another direction before he might ask her about Greta.

''Well, nothing concrete as yet, but I think it's negotiable.''

''And you're an able negotiator.''

''Thanks for that vote of confidence. You know I like talking to you. You give me the boost I need.

So tell me, are you going to be home tomorrow night, so I can call you again?''

''Is that a subtle way to find out if I have a date or not?'' she asked wryly.

''No, of course not,'' he protested. ''I just don't want to say something personal to your answering machine.''

''You mean like, How are you?'' she teased, smothering a giggle by pressing her hand against her lips.

''No, silly. Like I've been thinking about you all day, and wishing very much that I was with you right now.''

''I'd stay home by the phone to hear something as nice as that. Is that what you're going to tell me tomorrow night?''

''Something on that order—maybe a few things more,'' he added enticingly.

At that moment, Mickey came in from the outside with Alex. Kristi held a finger to her lips to caution him not to speak. ''Till tomorrow then,'' she said into the phone. Then, following it with a quick *good night*, she hung up.

Mickey came over to her. ''Were you talking to your boyfriend?'' he asked, a frown puckering his inquisitive eyes.

''That was Chad. He called to say he misses us.''

Mickey seemed relieved to hear it was Chad and

not Derek that she was talking to. "I bet he was spooked about what happened to Red Ott."

Kristi hesitated, nibbling the corner of her lip. "I—I decided not to tell him. In fact, I even sort of fibbed a little, because I knew it would upset him. You see, finding out Greta was gone might have made him decide he should come home right now—before he finished his business and everything. We wouldn't want him to do that, now would we?"

"Golly—no way would he need to do that. Anyhow, you can take care of me as good as Greta."

"Well, almost as good I bet," she said, putting her arms around him and giving him a good bear hug. "Now go get your shower and put on your pajamas while I fix up a bed for you."

"Yeah, where am I going to sleep in your house?" he asked, cocking his head up at her like a saucy blue jay. "I had a sleeping bag at home, but of course I didn't bring it here with me."

"Well, you're in luck, Mickey. You see, my couch in there in the living room pulls out and makes a great bed. And Alex likes it because it sets low on the floor. He'll probably jump on it and curl up at the end by your feet and sleep there with you. Will that bother you?"

"Golly, no!" he exclaimed emphatically. "That'll be really super."

*   *   *

The next two days passed quickly. Greta called early on Thursday morning to tell Kristi that Eric was bringing her back and that she'd be at Chad's by noon. She reported that her grandson was out of danger, although his condition remained serious. He would have to be in the hospital for three or four more days, and she planned to go back to Lancaster to help take care of him after he came home. For now, however, she wanted to get Chad's house in order, and have a good dinner ready for his return.

Knowing Greta would be there to get Mickey from school was really going to help Kristi out. Now she could leave directly from work to go pick up Chad at the airport. His plane wasn't due until five-fifty, and since it was only a twenty-minute drive from the Word Wise office, she arrived thirty minutes early.

Kristi didn't know why she was so keyed up, but she wandered around the endless corridors, back and forth, because she couldn't sit still. She even counted the flags lining the balcony, and watched the various people coming and going.

From time to time she stared at the arrival schedule, willing it to indicate the arrival of Chad's flight from Chicago. Finally it did, and almost immediately the announcement crackled loudly over the public address system. She quickly moved to a spot where she could see the passengers come down the ramp from the plane.

The first thing she noticed was Chad's sandy hair a bit above the other passengers' heads due to his six-foot-plus height. Next she saw his sun-tanned face and those blue, blue eyes, and everything around her faded away into nothingness.

She saw only Chad now—his lean, straight body, his casual, easygoing stride. With his jacket slung over his shoulder, he moved forward, looking and searching the crowd.

All she was aware of was him, his face, and the light that sprang up in his eyes as his searching gaze met hers, causing her heart to lurch crazily.

He strode toward her and the next thing she knew she was in his arms, wrapped up so tightly against him that she could barely breathe, her face pressed close to his chest, so she could hear the solid beating of his heart. After a moment, Chad lifted her face and kissed her hard, then put her away from him a little, looking down at her and smiling.

"I like having you here to meet me."

"I told you I would."

"I know. It just feels especially nice to me." He pulled her close again and kissed her, more gently this time. Then he released her, picked up his jacket that had slid to the ground, and slung it back over his shoulder. He looked at her with a

deep glitter in his eyes and his hand reached out
and touched her mouth.

"This is a public place, and I'll behave," he
said softly. "Let's get out of here." He picked up
his carry-on pack and they started toward the exit.

In the airport parking lot, Kristi fished her car
keys out of her shoulder bag and held them out to
Chad. "Do you want to drive?" she asked.

He shook his head. "Why would I want to keep
my eyes on the highway when I can sit back and
look at you?" His gaze roved, and lazily appraised
her, then he gave her a roguish wink and climbed
into the passenger side of her car.

She laughed. "Aren't you the smooth-talking
one. I take it from your antics and high spirits that
your business came through in Chicago."

"Did it ever! Best deal I've made for the company this year," he boasted.

"That calls for a celebration."

"I thought so too. And I've already planned one
for tonight—with a little help from Greta to pull
it off, of course." There was a bright ring of merriment in his voice as he told her this.

"How did you manage to set this up for tonight,
when you were in Chicago until right now?" she
asked uneasily. She had hoped to have the chance
to explain everything to Chad before he found out
that she'd kept what had taken place here a secret
from him. Undoubtedly, if he'd talked to Greta,

however, he knew the true facts. She stole a quick glance at him, but his mild expression told her nothing.

"Oh, I talked to Greta earlier today, and we worked out all the details. She and Mickey are going out for pizza and then taking in the new Disney movie. You and I, on the other hand, are going to have dinner at my place and a long talk."

"Oh." Kristi's voice spiraled and she looked at Chad questioningly. "What sort of long talk?" she asked suspiciously.

"A very interesting and important one, I'd say."

She accelerated and zipped along the turnpike without talking for several minutes. The next time she looked at him, she thought that something in his expression had changed, almost imperceptibly, and her heart beat against her ribs in an uneasy rhythm.

"I expect you're sort of mad at me, aren't you?" she said finally.

"Why on earth would I be mad at you?" He sounded genuinely perplexed.

"Because I didn't tell you Monday night about Greta having to leave to go to her grandson, and Mickey being with me. I thought you'd worry. I hope you understand."

"I do understand, Kristi. In fact, that's one of the important things I want to talk about." There was a slight emotional tremor in his voice that seemed familiar. She thought about it for a moment before she realized that Chad's voice had held that same sound when he'd leaned into the car that night and said *I love you.*

What was happening here, she wondered. Chad's words, his expression, in fact his whole manner seemed different to her. From that first moment in the airport when he'd scooped her up and hugged and kissed her in such an unrestrained way, his actions had been unusual. She was intrigued by this, and naturally excited by his show of affection. But she couldn't help but feel somewhat unnerved by it too. Before, when Chad said he had something important to talk about, it had always concerned Mickey. This time, because of the way Chad was behaving, the thought flashed through her mind that it just could be about her. . . .

Kristi could see Greta's handiwork all through Chad's house when she and Chad walked in. The furniture was dusted and polished, the carpets freshly swept, and Greta had the table in the dining area set for two, with a pair of ivory-colored candles waiting to be lit. She'd even placed a matchbook at Chad's place so he'd remember to light them to give the table setting a romantic glow.

When they entered the sparkling clean kitchen, there was a freshly baked peach pie on the counter, and beside it a note in Greta's neat handwriting detailing the seafood casserole she'd prepared for them that was stored in the refrigerator ready to be heated in the microwave.

"Goodness, Greta has gone to a lot of trouble to fix a fancy meal for you and me," Kristi said, eyeing the casserole and the fresh spinach salad that was in a glass bowl beside it.

"She wanted to do something special for you, for all you did for her, Kristi. You should have heard how pleased she was when I told her my plans for tonight. Greta really likes you, you know."

"I like her too. She's a jewel, and she looks at Mickey as her number-three grandson, I think."

Chad smiled. "I think he feels he is too."

"While we're talking about Greta and her grandsons, I want to say that I'm not only glad, but relieved that you aren't put out with me for not telling you right off about Greta having to leave Monday night and all. Thanks for being so understanding." She gave a soft sigh and smiled at him.

A return smile touched his mouth with sensual warmth. "My understanding is only half of it, Kristi. I'm happy about it. You see, the fact that you didn't want anything to worry me, or distract me from the business deal I was eager to accomplish in Chicago showed me something that's of the greatest importance to me. Something that means more than you could possibly know.'' He was looking at her intently and there was a heart-rending tenderness in his gaze.

''What's that? What do you mean?'' she asked, staring at him, totally confused by what he was saying.

''It showed me that you understand me. That you care enough about me to want to do whatever you can to make things work out well for me. You're my understanding partner. Isn't that right?''

''Well—of course I—I like to help you—any-way I can,'' she stammered.

''And you do care about me, don't you.'' It was more of a statement than a question, and Chad didn't wait for her to answer. ''I love you and everything about you, Kristi. You just have to dis-cover that you love me too. Love me enough to marry me and take on Mickey with me. We're a package deal, I'm afraid.''

She was stunned by his words, and her breath caught in her throat so she couldn't speak even if she'd wanted to. She didn't. She was afraid to say what she knew she must. She stood very still there in the middle of the kitchen. Chad took her in his arms, and his lips caressed her cheek. ''This is what I meant to talk to you about,'' he said softly. ''I intended to build up to it slowly and carefully, not blurt it out all at once like this. Did I jump the gun and spoil it?''

She shook her head. "Oh no—it's just such a surprise. I—I never expected anything like this," she said, fighting to gain control of her emotions.

"You should have. Surely you could see that I was falling more in love with you with every day that passed. And I honestly believe that you love me some too, but for some reason you won't admit it." He moved her away from him a little so he could look into her eyes. "Is it because of that Derek fellow? Do you think you're in love with him?" Chad's voice was rough with anxiety.

"No, absolutely not." She was very emphatic about it. "There's nothing between Derek and me. You're the one who's important to me, and I do care for you, more than anyone else ever. But—"

"No. There are no buts. If you love me, then surely you can see that we belong together. We're meant for each other. I love you. You love me. We both love Mickey. It's so right, Kristi," Chad said, placing his warm hands on her face to keep her from turning away. "Ours could be a love story made in heaven. Don't you know that?" Their eyes met as he spoke, his probing, hers dark with uncertainty.

"Please, Chad, there's something more, something I'm afraid you may not even realize." Her voice broke miserably. "We have to talk about it, but I can't do it standing here. Let's go to the living room and sit down, where we can discuss it calmly.'' She turned away as she said this, for tears were pushing into her eyes. She was filled with so many conflicting emotions, and she was at a loss as to how to handle any of them.

Was she being a total fool? she wondered. She was so completely in love with Chad, and now he was saying he loved her, and asking her to be his wife. Wasn't this what she'd dreamed of, even prayed would happen? It was everything she wanted, so why was she about to throw away her chance of happiness with the only man she'd ever really loved?

Kristi fought back her tears and, with her hands clenched tightly and pressed against her sides, she walked ahead of Chad into the living room. The answer was simple. It was the right thing to do.

They both sat down on Chad's burgundy leather couch, but Kristi sat at one end, angling her body so she could look at Chad as she talked and also keep a little distance between them.

''Looks like we're all set up for a good heart-to-heart talk. Although I'd prefer to sit closer to you so I could gaze into your beautiful eyes and hold your hand,'' Chad said, his tone faintly teasing.

She held her hand out to ward him off. ''No, you stay right where you are and hear me out.''

His expression sobered. "You make this sound awfully serious." His frown deepened. "I hope you're not going to tell me something I won't like to hear."

"It's important, Chad, important to both of us. And it may be something that hasn't occurred to you."

"All right—I'm listening." He leaned back and crossed his arms across his chest.

"Well . . . You remember that it was right after I rented the duplex that Mickey came."

Chad nodded. "Yeah, I was out of town and you took him in out of the rain."

"Right. Actually it was my getting involved with Mickey that sort of started our relationship." She paused, smiling softly. "You and me and Mickey started doing things together. We had such good times, the three of us. We soon cared a lot about each other. Don't you agree?" she asked, looking at him thoughtfully.

"Of course I agree!" He exclaimed emphatically. "I think you were more smitten with Mickey than with me. I discovered that I had to compete for your affections with a nine-year-old rival." He chuckled to himself, seeming to be amused recalling those earlier summer days.

Kristi chuckled too. "I was growing very fond of both you and Mickey, and you knew I was. I believe it was because of how we all cared for each other that made you think you might be in love with me.''

''Might be? Hey, I *am* in love with you, angel. That's already an established fact.'' He sat forward, acting like he was going to move closer to her.

Kristi held up her hand again. ''Hold on a minute! There's a bit more to say about this. I need to point out something important that you may not even realize.''

Chad looked puzzled. ''What's that?''

''I believe that even before you learned that Jack Wyatt was in the Witness Protection Program, you felt that Mickey would stay with you permanently.''

He shrugged. ''Of course I did. You know that.''

''And because of that, when you saw Sybil's negative reaction to this, it convinced you that the kind of woman you were looking for had to be one who could love Mickey as if he were her own— like me—''

''Now you hold on,'' he said, interupting her. ''I would never even speak of Sybil in the same breath as you. I never felt anything for her, and never would have, with or without Mickey. I've told you that.''

She nodded. ''I know that, Chad. But the fact remains that because of Sybil, without even realizing it, you've made yourself believe you want to marry me because I'd be right for Mickey.''

Chad instantly closed the space between them, placing his hands firmly on her shoulders and scrutinizing her face. ''Now you listen to me, Kristi—and listen good. I didn't have to make myself believe anything. Because nothing was ever clearer to me than the positive and irrevocable fact that I love you with an intensity I've never experienced before. It fills my heart, my mind, all of me.'' With this, his arms enfolded her, and his warm mouth moved over hers, ardent with passion, igniting a glorious response within her. Every nerve, every cell of her body responded to his touch. Chad's declaration of love sang in her heart, and her senses reeled at the depth of emotion Chad evoked in her, making her understand that their love for each other was genuine, and it was right.

When their kiss ended, Chad eased her away only far enough to be able to look into her eyes. ''You do believe that I truly adore you, don't you?'' he asked, his voice husky with emotion.

''Yes—I do now,'' she answered with a soft sigh, looking at him with love and joy shining out of her eyes.

Chad's expression was one of pure elation. ''And I'm going to love you every minute of every day for the rest of my life, Kristi. That I promise you.''

"Is that every single day—rain or shine?" she asked, laughing happily as she reached up to circle her arms around his neck.

Chad's strong arms immediately folded her close against him again. "Rain or shine, my darling. Rain or shine!"